THE PARTISAN

by

FENEK SOLÈRE

Skylore Books
2022

Hardcover ISBN: 978-1-64264-184-4
Paperback ISBN: 978-1-64264-185-1

For B.D.

'And in the shock of the battle the men
   of the North stood
one close to another, forming as it were
   a bulwark of ice . . .'

Continuatio Hispana
Isidore of Beja
754 CE

CONTENTS

PART ONE

PART ONE

𝔫𝟪𝟪

They kicked down the door, emptying AKs indiscriminately into the crowded auditorium. As security personnel fell or scattered, the insurgents advanced behind a flash of light, their faces black balaclavas, sliding magazines into the maws of their guns, tricolor badges sewn onto khaki lapels.

The reception screen shattered in a spider-web of glass and dangling wires, causing the Pan Eurabia banner to flutter and fall. Semtex drum beats pounded away, echoing in the maze of corridors above, where the families of ruling party delegates barred doors and hid children under beds. Later, witnesses described a fair skinned man with a Glock 40, barrel tilted downward, firing directly into the faces of National Assembly Deputies—men who had signed the *Treaty for the Union of the Mediterranean*, effectively paving the way for the North African colonisation of Europe. Others recalled diners diving behind overturned tables, white-shirted waiters scythed like wheat in Picardie. Most survivors identified a small female in a leather hipster jacket as the ringleader, strutting around, barking commands, shepherding the white families gently to one side, herding the Africans, Fifth Columnists, and miscegenators towards the toilets. Holding a Chinese AK 56 in the proper position, her small hand on the fore grip and the wooden stock wedged in place by her left shoulder, she repeated her catechism. Before her, scurrying in her cross-hairs, mothers and fathers huddled in an effort to shield crying children behind their legs, the smell of ammonia and urea tingling in their nostrils.

'This is for Juillac!' she yelled. A faint smile and her index finger squeezed mechanically on the trigger, loosing a spray of 7.6 mm shells, bodies collapsing, fat babies slipping like spinning tops in the ballet dance of bouncing bullets on bloodied tiles. The phantom legion were shouting 'Vive la France, Vive la nation!,' before melting away as quickly as they came, *black sun* calling cards spilling from their pockets . . .

*

The news coverage was global. Conspiracy theories went viral. At first the authorities were unsure how to respond. Should they kill-switch the virtual media, conduct mass arrests as before? They had worried at the escalation in violence ever since the forced clearances in the Gironde and the compulsory seizure of land in the Dordogne. But with the first wave of deportations to the camps in the *Massif Central* came a huge backlash. They had never anticipated such unprecedented terrorism. Questions were being asked at the highest levels. Would the docile French really fight back? Had years of brainwashing proved insufficient? Analyses carried out by the Rainbow Government's Policy Institute had not predicted this. All the planning was thrown into doubt. The transition process was now rapidly escalating towards the tipping point. No outcome, other than the dispossession of the native inhabitants was imaginable to the oligarchs in the Elysées. Could they have miscalculated? Clearly there were people militant enough to fight and die for the Old France. So, with body counts rising and iconic venues and major cities being throttled in a grip of panic, the reptilian Minister of Interior Justice, Said Ben Hassi, stepped forward into the flicker of journalists' cameras to announce the regime's crack-down on this latest wave of anti-state terror.

'This is a national emergency,' he declared in a grating Moroccan accent, 'These are sick and twisted people who will to stop at nothing to end our equal society.' Then, with tears welling in his eyes, he lifted a WANTED poster up to the camera, 'Look,' he breathed, 'One of their ringleaders is a woman.' His twitching fingers raised a photograph. And suddenly, for the first time, in every home across the nation, the pretty face of a dark-haired girl stared back defiantly at her people, challenging them to rise up. 'I tell you, this woman, this - *Pétroleuse* must be stopped . . .'

*

Driving down Rue Tronchet with a machined assault rifle across her lap, the girl in question was giving instructions.

'Use the pentaerythritol tetranitrate devices,' she was saying, 'By now the Foreign Minister's Air Burkina flight to Ouagadougou will be over the sea!'

Once past the Gare Saint-Lazare they stopped and shot at three armed Europol militia troopers standing under the clock tower on the forecourt. The guards had been ordered to harass travellers entering and leaving the city, checking their identity papers, enforcing the diversity quotas imposed when allocating tickets to the occupants of premier and second class carriages. The firefight had been short but intense. *La pétroleuse* had charged across the open space, leading her men, raking the militia with SMGs. One of her companions fell wounded.

'Carry him!' she bellowed, 'we leave no one behind for these scum!'

Then, pulling away from the station they turned down Rue d'Amsterdam and passed under the giant advertisements for the Eid-al-Kabir festival, smashing the windows of a new Shari'ah branch of BNP Paribas before tossing a Molotov cocktail into a ground-floor office. The fire shot up through the building, setting off sprinklers and pulsing red alarms that drew police sirens like moths to light. Having set their trap, the gang filed out of the stolen Skoda and waited in the darkness of surrounding doorways, barrels poised, ready to unleash death into the street. They intended to kill as many officials as they could before scattering through Pigalle, disappearing under the shadow of the minarets.

*

Back at the Ministry in the Place Vendome, Ben Hassi was being informed by his stylish private secretary, Alphonse Belan, that an Airbus 330-200 had just been vapourised three hundred kilometres west of the Balearics. The minister's acne-pitted complexion oozed sebum. His head twisted, open pores gaping like screaming mouths in a torture chamber. 'Get me Levangie. Now!' he shouted, with a sweep of his arm. 'I want all our resources focused on locating the perpetrators.'

'Minister,' Belan mouthed quietly, gesturing to the Nokia in his hand, recognising the source of the incoming communication, 'it's Monsieur le President. For you.'

Ben Hassi coughed, clearing his throat before taking the call. He stood rigidly, then, clutching the phone in his left hand, he listened intently to President Ahmed Baya of Tunisia. The French Foreign Minister was the President's brother in law, so avenging his murder was a matter of honour.

'Yes, Mr President, we will do all in our power. This girl is one of the key conspirators. She seems to have a loyal following among the *kufar*. We will hunt her down. Please don't worry.' Then, listening attentively to Baya's response, 'You want her brought alive to Tunis?' Ben Hassi smiled into the receiver, 'I understand, you need it to be like the old times,' he laughed, images of white slaves filling his mind.

After hanging up, Ben Hassi turned to Belan, slipped off his suit jacket, picked up some bottled water, and walked pensively in his sweat stained shirt towards the Louis XIV desk overlooking Rue Cambon, saying, 'Looks like we have a civil war on our hands, Alphonse. Get me President Belaire at the Elysées and then Levangie and that damned Operations Commander of his.'

Liberté, Égalité, Fraternité!

Despite the late hour, Ben Hassi was still in his office, fuelled by endless coffees. Alphonse would every fifteen minutes or so mince over to the windows overlooking the square. At the courtyard's far end were the ornamental wrought iron gates, each bearing the coat of arms of the Republic side by side with a newly welded crescent moon. Two *gendarmes* stood on sentry duty, machine guns at the ready, their eyes glancing occasionally over to the anti-vehicle trap buried in the gravel. Belan watched the headlights moving along Boulevard des Capucines and saw the lasers shining on the newly constructed Rainbow Bridge spanning the Seine, emblematic of two continents coming together. He was clicking his tongue in exasperation. The Head of the State Security Service and his operative were late.

'You know,' said Alphonse, 'things are so much better now than before.' Then, holding his hands together almost in prayer, 'All our peoples are coming together in a true melting-pot of colours, faiths, and sexual orientations.' His voice was wistful, 'I can see a time when prejudice will end.'

Ben Hassi smiled benevolently. What possible future could this effeminate man expect under a caliphate France, he wondered. Was he naïve, self-loathing, or just plain stupid?

When wiry Claude Levangie and the pinch-faced Auguste Fouvier, breathless and confused, finally arrived at the Minister's office, it was nearly 3 o'clock by the ormolu clock on the mantelpiece. Levangie had served with honour in Bosnia Herzegovina, back-channelling guns and money to the Muslim Brothers to prevent the Serbs penetrating the Lasva valley towards Travnik. Based in a small headquarters in Bjelobuce on the edge of Turbe he had dealt first hand with young jihadists now gaining positions of authority among the immigrants in the newly reconstituted French state. Up until recently the ever-thoughtful Fouvier had been head of the Middle-East Bureau, working closely with the Soros Foundation to ferment the Arab Spring, before being recalled to deal with the threat from indigenous terrorist groups. Alphonse took their hats and coats, slipping them decorously over an outstretched arm and swept out of the room with a flourish just as the recent arrivals took chairs opposite Ben Hassi.

'What do we know about this girl?' demanded Ben Hassi.

'Her name is Sabine D'Orlac,' said Levangie. She is twenty-two and was born in Sarthe.'

'Motivation?'

'Originally revenge, her mother's flat in Le Mans was burnt out by some Sudanese.'

'And now?'

'Ideological. She has been cohabiting with Luc Dubois for some time.'

'Dubois. Yes, his name appears in this file.' The minister tapped the folder in front of him.

'A fanatic, sir,' Fouvier interjected, 'He is a law student at Assas 2 and leads a militant faction.'

'You seem to know a lot about these two little mosquitoes.'

'At one time we had a mole inside their circle.'

'At one time?'

Fouvier and Levangie looked at each other with some embarrassment.

'She went native,' Levangie replied, reluctantly.

'Turned?'

'Oui'

'Is that normal?'

'Not exactly. Dominique Pascale was a good agent.'

'So why?'

'Because these people are themselves exceptional.' The minister shook his head.

'Why use a woman for such a job?'

'Our psychologists profiled D'Orlac and categorised her as a closet lesbian.'

Ben Hassi exploded, 'What do you think this is? A Stieg Larsson novel? This woman isn't some fictional Lisbeth Salander!'

'With respect, Minister . . .'

Ben Hassi brushed the comment away, 'What is she like?'

Dedicated, fit, and merciless. We know she masterminded the failed attempt to assassinate Belaire last month. Our people tell us she did some theatrical work in the past and is a consummate actress, a chameleon.'

'A Scarlet Pimpernel!'

'We seek him here. We seek him there. We seek
that damned Pimpernel everywhere . . .'

'And we have no one on the inside to tell us
which role she is playing at the moment?'

'Sir, we found our last insider decapitated in the
back of a garbage truck in Colombey-les-Deux-
Eglises in the Haute-Marne.'

'They are that good?'

'There are counter intelligence specialists in sympathy with them.'

'They have people inside our department?'

'That is distinctly possible.'

'I see!' Ben Hassi's sausage fingers tapped again
at the file. These two are a danger to us. He must be
killed. She must be made an example.'

'Do you have a plan, Minister?'

'Money of course! Money buys us information.
Many of these cockroaches are poor, surely money
talks?'

'It does and we have had some limited success
with that particular tactic.'

'But?'

'Their nativist message is attractive!' The Minister's eyes flashed amber but Levangie continued,
anxious to make his point, 'Their credo is proving
popular.'

'What credo?'

'That Europe is being swamped by outsiders as
distinctly different from Europeans as men from
monkeys!'

'That is racist.' Levangie rubbed his chin.

'It is their way of thinking.'

'It excludes people like me,' said the Moroccan.
Fouvier rubbed tired eyes as Ben Hassi spoke, trying
to mask his contempt for politically correct platitudes.

'Minister, the truth is we cannot get any closer to D'Orlac or Dubois than we can to their commanders Arnaud Bellew or Franck Bodine, it's as if they wear a cloak of invisibility and hundreds of thousands are complicit in their criminal activities.'

'We got those ecoterrorists, so why not these?'

'Oh, we will get them, Minister, but I am just not sure how or when,' Levangie confirmed. The shirt-sleeved official raised a cup.

'So gentlemen, tell me what I need to make available to you so that we can achieve this objective?' Ben Hassi then continued, 'Before that is, our beloved and very recently deceased Foreign Minister's loving sister persuades the President of Tunisia to cut off my balls!'

'I want to hand-pick a team of twelve from across all services!' Fouvier quickly asserted before his boss could countermand him.

'You have my permission.'

'And I want to bring in a British specialist.' Levangie shifted uncomfortably in his chair.

'James bond?' The Minister's eyebrow arched.

'John Costello.'

'Why this man?'

'I worked with him a few years ago in Cairo and was very impressed.'

'Do what you think best, but get her, do you hear me? I want her taken alive by Muharram.'

Both security men nodded.

'She will be our priority.'

'And by the way,' Ben Hassi added, 'get a covert message out to the resistance through your most reliable sources that unless they surrender Dubois and D'Orlac by noon tomorrow we will begin weekly executions of their comrades in prison.'

Both visitors winced.

'That is not the French way!' Levangie dared breathe.

'I am not French and this is now a Eurabic State,' said the Minister.

After Levangie and Fouvier had departed Ben Hassi's mind drifted back to his own youth, living in the Goutte d'or. His teenage years were haunted by his father's political activity. Ali Ben Hassi had been amongst those that led the Algerian civil rights movement onto the Neuilly Bridge in October '61. There they were caught between the Police troopers and the CRS. Systematically beaten and then killed in the frenzied hand-to-hand fighting, Ali's body fell battered and senseless like so many others into the Seine.

The minister recalled the newspaper headlines the next morning: 'MOSLEM RIOTERS BURN PARIS'. He had sworn then as he accompanied his mother to the hospital morgue that the French would pay for what they had done. Spirited out of France and back to Oran, he joined the Muslim Brotherhood, determined to take his revenge at any cost, raising the Qur'an with the incantation 'Allahu Akbar!'

*

The members of the Revolutionary Council of the Resistance slipped away from the Quai de l'Horloge in the early hours, out onto the big empty boulevards and wide avenues where the nation's ancient buildings had fallen into disrepair. Beams of sunlight swam across the Seine's torpitude as dawn broke over the *city of light* and the men and women split up, one covering the other's back with snub-nosed 45's under damp gaberdine. They made their way in the rain; through the districts that had seen hard times. Passing old houses, porches with bow-ers, flower gardens, and Christian graveyards churned over by decades of demands for special privileges from immigrant minorities. They had all read about the exorbitant cost of welfare to pay for dysfunctional black families, the frequent sealing off of areas due to swamp fever quarantines. Now they walked through them.

For the last few years whole areas of the city had been governed by tribal and religious warlords. There were 'no go' areas in all the urban centres, not only in the slums. The black shadow stretched out across suburbia. Just arriving in any provincial city by bus or train meant crawling through a deafening cacophony of horns, throngs, swarms, welcoming and bidding farewell to relatives from South Asia. The kerbs covered by sellers of tomatoes, cucum-bers, kebabs, and children screaming for baksheesh.

In recent months the movement had it on good authority that *Yersinia pestis* DNA had been found in Marseilles; the deadly bacillus that had carried the plague to Europe thrived once again on French soil. And of course there was the news about the writing off of all Third World debt, regardless of an unsurpassed African talent for profligacy.

Dissension had began innocuously enough when some, like Laurent Bardet, a successful corporate lawyer whose phrases exploded off his tongue like fireworks, began raising his voice about civil rights for whites. But then large-scale arrests started, especially when the economy polarised the communities. By then the police and military hierarchy had been largely replaced by commissars of all complexions, fixated on the objective of universal bi-racialism. Isolated and elderly whites, already the victims of frequent assaults, were sub-jected to daily ignominies as they went out to collect meagre pensions. The country's traditions, festivals and rites were being overwhelmed by those of other religions. Even as the members of the patriot's revolutionary council made their clandestine exit, there were the pink banners, bobbing balloons, and glossy leaflets calling for a further reduction in the age of consent from the previous day's Gay Pride march still blowing through Chaillot.

Fearing public unrest the state had immediately imposed curfews, crackdowns, and confiscations, describing the activities of some anti-government activists as 'Neo-Nazi.' It had soon become apparent to everyone that they were being politically, economically, and racially replaced wholesale. When the government began requisitioning trains and removing large numbers of white Frenchmen to camps in the mountains, allegedly because there was insufficient food and electricity to sustain populations in the cities, there was panic. The government's justification, that they did not want to separate vulnerable immigrants from their home communities, despite the fact that some of these immigrants were second or third generation incomers and still could not speak French, rang hollow.

Of course all the TV channels covered up the true nature of these resettlements and vilified anyone and everyone who complained that the French were at the back of the queue. Crime elicited the same response and frequent outbreaks of TB, cholera, and other infectious diseases were explained as the consequence of poverty and inequity. The news presenters decried the nativist response as vigilantism and racism, showcasing bug-eyed brown orphans, insisting they deserved help. But now the growing membership of the New Resistance came from all parts of society.

II.S9:10/09

efore noon the following day Ben Hassi's first victim, a middle-aged man, was led in an orange one-piece jumpsuit by a rope out into the militia garrison's main courtyard, in Saint-Armand-Montrond. Jean Maran had up until recently been a professor of politics living quietly with his family near Sancerre. He had first come to the judiciary's attention when he published some well-received academic papers on critics of Enlightenment thinking like Frederic Le Play and Emile Keller. Ever mindful to control and regulate the curriculum, the local authorities had become alarmed by his public support for the Counter Revolutionary Tradition and accused him of expressing anti-government sentiments in front of his students. Though they had fabricated the issue as a pretext, when the local police searched his house they found resistance literature by Guillame Faye and research papers relating to François-René de La Tour du Pin. Incensed by such thinking, the public prosecutor had ordered the material's immediate confiscation and confirmed Maran's confinement. His wife of ten years, and his two children, a boy and a girl, afraid for their safety, had immediately disowned him. Now, ten months after his trial, as he was being frog-marched to his death, Maran scuffed his ill-fitting rubber shoes into the red gravel.

'To hell with you,' he shouted, '*Vive La Pétroleuse! Vive la Résistance!*'

Jean's hands were bound unceremoniously behind him with thick cord and his slight body was pushed back against the wall. Twenty metres away six Zouave soldiers stood in a ragged line, rifles at the ready. Then, the linen blindfold was pulled down over his eyes. He listened as the officer in charge told his men to take aim and fire. He heard the discharge as he fell, buffeted by the impact. The taciturn captain dispatched him with a *coup-de-grace*.

*

'The money's not for me, you understand,' insisted *La Pétroleuse*, raising a Ruger 38SP into the clerk's eyeline, 'It's for the liberation of our people!' Five sets of nervous fingers were stuffing cash into linen pillows while customers lay face down on the bank's cold tiles. '*Plus vite, plus vite!*' she said, as she gestured to a man in a black hat and long winter coat sweeping a Mossberg 30-30 over their heads.

'Still all clear,' he said, glancing out through blinds onto the Rue Scribe. *La Pétroleuse* signalled for the others to take the bulging pillows to the motorcycles. The man with the Mossberg pulled open the front door and watched as his compatriots rushed out to load their money into large panniers.

Then calling to the girl who was placing a laser-printed notice on the screen above the counter, they sped off on roaring V2 engines.

When the police came later, they tore down *La Pétroleuse*'s message:

> We will seize the bankers' assets
> and distribute their ill-gotten gains
> to alleviate the suffering they have caused

La Pétroleuse

A barefoot figure pirouetted over the rain-swept cobbles towards John Costello. There was a crooked lurch to her limbs and she hugged a bottle of brandy like a suckling child to full white breasts. Surreptitiously watching, as the streetlights's neon blur refracted like dew off her black stockings, the British Special Air Services agent saw for the first time through the sheen of Parisian blue those two young but simultaneously ancient Celtic eyes, all shiny and walnut brown.

He meant to intercept her, try to engage her in conversation, confirm this was the Robin Hood character he had been hunting for months, but at that moment a blaze of chrome yellow screeched around the corner, coming to a halt just short of its destination. The taxi driver pressed on his horn with irritation as passengers spilled out of swinging doors—hard young bodies rushing for the club's gaping shutters. The bewildered girl stood dead still in the middle of the road, face set, looking belligerent, and then thumped down hard on the bonnet with a clenched fist, sending plumes of droplets spiralling up into the air.

'*Merde!*' she yelled, throwing a single finger salute at the Congolese cursing back at her from behind two slashing windscreen wipers. 'Fucking foreigners,' she screamed, 'we shouldn't give you licences!'

If a policeman had seen the incident, she would have been arrested on the spot for displaying racial intolerance, but, surprisingly, there was no one around in uniform. Not even one of the 'Specials,' recently formed units charged with infiltrating public events to ensure participants adhered to the new ethnicity codes. Turning, the girl staggered away in the opposite direction, still shouting profanities, waving the vehicle on with a sword-swipe sneer. Then, suddenly, from somewhere in the dark, a camera's digital flash blinded her. She staggered, swerving like a skier cut loose from the drag of a motorboat, stumbling awkwardly through a crowd of revellers and tripping over the kerb.

Costello stood, watching the whole scene, leaning against a lamppost in a long green raincoat. He raised his hands to cup a cigarette and must have taken his eyes off her for a moment, because in the next instant she was reeling up close, the wild jig-a-jagging motion of her hips colliding against him side on. He tried to reach out, but too late: her balance thrown, bone to bone sent her sprawling down onto hands and knees. The glass infant slipped and shattered, shooting splinters. He thought she looked shocked, mouth like a gasping fish, her natural reactions slowed by alcohol. By the time the girl's disbelieving expression had become fixed on the ground before her the brandy had all but drained away between the cobbles, leaving her nails to claw desperately at shards of glass.

He threw away his cigarette and bent down, extending a helping hand. The crouching figure was coughing and distraught, a thread of saliva trailing from her mouth. At first she ignored him, squatting inert. Then the tips of his fingers accidently brushed through her hair and glided down the curve of her neck. He became conscious of feminine softness and a rising tide of PC guilt swept over him, negative feelings associated with an intrusion of her personal space.

'Sorry, can I help you?'

The girl tugged tails of wet hair from her face and stared up at him with feline contempt.

'Don't touch me!' she protested, with the faintest quiver of drawn lips. Her glance shot out like a switch blade, accusing eyes stabbing back at him. The moment carried the tension of a street mugging. He noticed a large piece of broken bottle in her hand and he moved back. 'Get away from me, you arsehole!'

'No harm intended,' he tried to reassure her, raising both hands.

Costello could tell she was prepared to use the shank. He also knew he could take her, but now was not the moment. First, he had to be sure this was *La Pétroleuse*. The girl threw her weapon aside, pushed up from the knees, rising slowly, tilting this way and that, straightening out her dress. When she had steadied herself she began hitting out with slapping palms and babbling incoherently about her precious booze. Her arms rotated like helicopter blades. When she got no response, she went at him even harder, screaming abuse in a Breton accent. He caught hold of her hands and forced them down to her sides.

'*Arrête, arrête!*'

She must have realised his French was poor and sensed the futility of her anger, because without warning the storm blew out, bare feet kicking uselessly into the air. She shrugged her shoulders and fell silent. Their eyes met. It was like standing in the centre of a tornado, air crackling and sparking with electrostatic energy. Before she could ask the obvious question, he had oranged the end of a Gitane and slipped it into the corner fold of her slurring mouth. A cloud of blue smoke obscured her face for an aeon as she took a drag. She then spat out the offending object. A dying circle of burning light bounced along the ground. Just for a second, he felt a tremor and thought the tantrums were coming back. Then, 'Got any American?' she asked.

Passing car headlights sent a cloud of grey feathery wings flapping skyward. The echo of an engine backfiring resounded off the dog turds lying like soft apostrophes in the gutters along the boulevard. 'You're English?'

'Close enough,' Costello replied. Her eyes dipped a fraction. The man knew she was buying time. He had spent months studying the renegade, desired by half of France. He brushed the back of his coat, seeking reassurance from the automatic at the base of his spine.

'It must have been one hell'va party?' he continued.

'Sorry?'

Costello pointed his cigarette towards the long line of youngsters being frisked by burly tuxedos.

'I didn't notice,' she said.

There was disappointment on her face. She slumped against wrought iron railings and let out a sigh.

He said, 'Where are your shoes?'

She smiled, 'I threw them at a bum in there!' As if to emphasise her point she swivelled on one foot and jabbed a red, broken thumbnail into the underbelly of air over her left shoulder. Eyes like saucers: 'And if the son of a bitch comes out here after me I'll throw yours at him too!'

Those eyes met his in an instant of recognition and she laughed, head rolling loosely across her shoulders. Costello watched her intently, evaluating her features against the photos he had seen in the dossier.

'You're a strange one,' she said, 'I thought you English were austere like Germans, but you seem . . . almost human.'

'Is that supposed to be a compliment?'

'Most French despise Germans!'

'Really?'

'Oui, in my experience that's the way it is. We're jealous of them.'

'But we're all Europeans'

'*Ah bon?*' She laughed, 'An Englishman saying he is European?'

'You don't seem convinced' He put a cigarette to his lips.

'I've never been convinced by anything except mankind's endless capacity for sin.'

'That sounds religious. Are you Catholic?'

''A Mohammedan convert like everyone else around here,' she beamed.

'Cynic!'

'Right then, what the hell else are you after, anyway?'

Costello craned his neck, took a long pull on his cigarette, telescoping the vast panorama of the stars. She watched in silence. He sensed this moment was crucial. He needed to spend time with her. She waited.

'Can you imagine that somewhere out there in space there are aliens looking straight back at us right now?' he said.

The girl let out a snort. They've already landed, take a look around you!'

'Can I walk you home?'

It sounded lame, but in her ears it sounded familiar, yet another man hitting on her and she accepted the ritual.

'Home!' she said, 'that is a joke?'

'Wherever then,' he added quickly, 'The police will pick you up here.'

Newspaper reports had been full of round-ups all week. Vans of bearded puritans robed in white had been sanctioned to drive around town in the early hours bundling offenders into the back of their vehicles.

She went quiet for a moment; then, a red spark ignited in her retina. 'Let's go to a little place I know, it's very close by.'

'Don't you think you've had enough?' He was trying to sound concerned rather than patronising, but was unsure of how it came out in his schoolboy French.

'My friend,' she said, 'I've had nowhere near enough. I could drink you under the table anytime!'

He draped his mackintosh over the little hunch made by her stiff rebellious shoulders. Costello was thinking where it would be best to make the 'snatch' once he was sure she was alone and unguarded. His men were not far away. She was chattering on in broken English about knowing where to go and who to meet.

'You'll see,' she said, 'I know this city very well.'

They walked arm in arm through a light shower of rain. He in his brown brogues and her in black sheer stockings. He held off contacting his team. It was a judgement call and for the first time in his career he made the wrong one. Afterwards, he would ask himself why. But at that moment it seemed the right thing to do. The warm balm of an Indian summer had rusted into autumn and now a first hint of frost was in the air. They took a battered taxi at L'Opera. Once out of sight of Des Poissonniers they crossed the late night Bazaar on the Rue Reamur and Rue de Rivoli, making for the channel cut by the river. In the doorway of a small church two old women wrapped in scarves were trying to sell root vegetables. She said she felt better now and wanted to walk. She revived in the soft breeze. There were few people on the Place du Chatelet. Just a derelict carousel from a Kazakh circus troop standing against the skyline and some blacks polluting the air with ragga and drug deals.

'Perhaps,' she said, pointing at the gaudy vans, 'some drunken woman has frightened the animals off?'

In the distance the sound of the *bateaux mouche* rolled along the length of the Seine, arc lights stretching upwards over the stone embankment, moths playing kiss-chase under the canopy of trees.

*

After cutting through back alleys she pointed to a cellar bar.

'We can get a drink in here!' she said, him pushing open the narrow door, her back disappearing into a dark, musty passageway.

Costello followed her, lump in throat, evaluating the potential for a trap, as they climbed down a creaking wooden staircase into a cavern. Below, cab drivers and tired, vampiric prostitutes lurked in twilight, vacant expressions staring at the football on the plasma screen hanging precariously from a beam to one side of the bar. It reminded him of a provincial railway station. They took up residence on red swivel chairs at the counter.

'*Pour vous?*' she asked her new acquaintance.

He looked at the array of bottles hanging from the metal optics.

'Whatever.'

'*Deux Jacques*', she called.

The Turkish owner waddled over, wearing a green waistcoat and a scimitar smile. A strong, hairy forearm filled their glasses. The first one was soon drained.

'Want another?' he asked.

'*S'il vous plaît*' she nodded. He beckoned to the tawny barman.

'Two more, make them doubles!'

'So anyway, what's your name?'

'John Sargent', he lied, 'And yours?'

'Camilla,' she reciprocated.

'Nice', he smiled. Costello knew that Sabine D'Orlac had recently been using the pseudonym Camilla Deboo, having assumed the identity of a former twenty-three year old Breton language teacher from Rennes who had quit her job and come to Paris on a modelling assignment.

'So Johnny—do you mind if I call you that? John sounds so plain and old.' She rolled his name on her tongue to force a laugh.

He duly obliged through gritted teeth, 'There's a song isn't there, *"Oui*, Johnny remember me" . . .'

'There is indeed,' his fingers played piano on the wooden bar, then he sang 'Yes, I'll always remember.' It was her turn to laugh.

'Tell me, what do you do?'

'I work in car insurance.'

'Sounds exciting!'

'It isn't, trust me. I am bored of the day-in-day-out routine.'

'So you've come to Paris to change your life, right?'

'Sort of,' he nodded.

'Well, this city is the centre of the world. Have you been here long?'

He knew she was playing with him. It was a game of cat and mouse.

'Just two weeks. And you, what's your story?'

She nodded and emptied her glass. He watched her click her fingers at the barman. She had short black hair and big drop earrings. When she lifted her third glass a gold ring suddenly deflated his growing erection.

'Me,' she feigned surprise that he was even remotely interested, 'I'm an actress. Between jobs. You understand?'

'Done anything I might have heard of?'

'Just one art house movie. Strictly low budget.' Costello affected shock. The look on his face said it all.

'It wasn't porn!' she insisted.

'So where do you live?'

'I have a studio in Montparnasse.'

'Sounds chic.'

'Not if you have to live there!' She waved that ring under his nose again. The tip of his penis was tingling. 'Emile thinks he is the new Picasso.'

'Emile?' Costello could only think that Luc Dubois was the Emile in question.

'The bastard with my shoes in his mouth!'

'Volatile relationship?'

'He's given me nothing but trouble. One useless year in hell!' Her hand reached for the Special Services man's pocket, 'I'll take that cigarette after all' she said, lighting up and blowing a long jet trail indulgently into his face. 'Now Johnny,' she purred, 'If you've got nothing better to do I'll tell you all about it?'

*

'So you see I am all out of luck. No job, no prospects. It's likely with this new census I'll be forced to go home.'

'New census?' Costello was fully aware of the Rainbow government's recent data survey and what it was intended for but decided to play dumb.

'*Oui*', she continued. They are repatriating people like me back to our regions of birth. They say it's all part of the new austerity programme to counter the financial deficit.'

'I had no idea.'

'Yes, I know some boys who have been deported. They had to report to the authorities and were forced to stand for hours in freight trains.'

After a while she stopped talking and lit another cigarette, sending two long plumes of smoke from flaring nostrils.

'Do you want another drink?' he asked. Costello felt he had her now. Reading between the lines this girl was steely and wily—her visage the perfect recruitment poster for the Resistance. She shot hot eyes over some newcomers hustling in around the bar.

'Let's get a table!'

They moved to a dark alcove. She sat there with her head propped in the palm of her hand. She was talking lasciviously in order to buy time and he was getting excited. Ten years of marriage had thwarted his ego. Costello could see her big brown eyes shining in the dull red glow of the wall light. Just for a second he was not sure if he should shoot her or fuck her.

'Are you sure you want to tell me all this?' he said.

She shrugged her shoulders nonchalantly.

'If I don't tell you it will just be someone else.'

John reached out for the ashtray and pushed it over to her. She flicked at the tip of her light. A tall man with a Jacques Mesrine-style moustache came into the bar. When he saw Johnny's companion, a flicker of fiendish recognition ran across his face and he peeled away from his friends to come stumbling through the chairs. From an adjacent table he tried to engage them in conversation.

'*Bonsoir* Brigitte,' he laughed, then raising his finger, 'Who's your new friend?'

'It's a secret, Henri,' she purred, pointing to the crushed cigarette wrapper on the table in front of her, 'And there's a price to pay for such information.'

Henri slapped his breast pocket and shook his head. 'I'm all out,' he squealed in a poor imitation of Vincent Cassel from *Public Enemy Number One*. The French girl turned away.

'Hey,' Henri said, trying win back her favour, 'If you think I'm drunk you should have seen Martin last night', his head rolled back in mock amazement, 'Unbelievable!'

The girl was unmoved and did not even look his way. John watched her thumb the empty cigarette box rigidly.

'Henri,' she said pointing at John, '*Nous étions parlant.*'

The man's face sobered up as he moved off his seat with a one-finger gesture of retreat. 'Bitch!' he spat, pulling up his waistband, revealing a sidearm. The Agent instinctively twitched, certain that any attempt to 'lift' his target in the narrow confines of the club would lead to a bloodbath that neither he or she would survive.

'Drunken jerk!' the girl hissed.

'A close friend of yours?' Costello asked, just controlling his muscular reflex. 'He seemed to have got you confused with someone else.'

'An acquaintance,' she corrected him, 'a spiv, a racketeer and he's drunk. Can't tell me from all the other girls!' John slipped a hand into his trouser pocket, ostensibly to fumble for change but really to switch on a tracker device.

The girl opposite him pointed a finger over to where the prostitutes were sitting. 'Interested in any shopping?'

'Not really,' he said, 'I've got other objectives.'

She laughed out loud once more. 'Now, if you've got money to buy me a vodka I'll continue . . .'

The escalator ground upwards like a defunct piece of farm machinery. In an old, empty station like Saint-Michel, the wind whirled about, ruffling her hair, sucking the tenuous trails of blue smoke coming off her cigarette skywards into the vaulted ceiling high above. It was just after midnight, one hour before the Caliphate's troopers had license to act. She noticed a few youngsters riding down towards her on the opposite side, their high-pitched laughter scratching metallically off the white ceramic tiles. Just ahead, a quiet, bourgeois, middle-aged couple, a fat woman and her skinny husband, argued poisonously among themselves. Behind her, taking two stairs at a time, a lone man in a long black leather coat, lank pony tail swinging loosely, was plugged into his iPod. His needle-thin legs, lost in outsize boots, followed her ascent to the street.

Stepping onto the concourse in her bare feet she was confronted by a black policeman leaning lazily on the shelf of a late night kiosk. The vendor's face behind the glass, lit by a flickering strip light, was perplexed and weary. A woman with a sleeping mulatto baby strapped to her chest pushed past a lonely man with the concave cheeks of a cocaine addict. Ahead, the orange haze from the streetlights was forcing itself down the black throat of Guimard's art noveau metro entrance.

Everything as normal, she was thinking, as her head began to clear. The familiar sordid sewer smell of decline was in her nostrils. The close attentions of Costello, however, had unnerved her. His unsolicited date had seemed natural enough at first but as she began to drink herself sober she knew what he was doing. After indulging him for a further thirty minutes she had excused herself to the toilet and slipped out of the window, stopping occasionally to check if she was being followed.

Rubbing her face, she looked up again and saw the paunchy policeman looking intently at her bare feet. He pushed himself off from the handrail, trying, she thought, to pick her out for questioning.

Nothing to be afraid of, she told herself. Cops saw this kind of thing all the time.

It was a good excuse for a bribe to avoid a ticket. The city was full of crazies, rich pickings these days. A wave of hot air gently brushed the back of her legs as a train pulled into a platform and she skipped past the officer with a smile. He tipped his hat with a fat finger and a lecherous whistle. In response she cast an appreciative backward glance and faked a plume of post-coital pleasure. It was enough for him. She heard a grunt as she started running up the steps and could imagine what was going on behind those piggy eyes as they slid all over her figure.

On the Petit Pont she stood for a moment catching her breath at the Seine's edge. She wavered, spread her arms on the parapet, looking over towards the looming shadow of Notre Dame.

That damn Englishman, she was thinking.

Car headlights tangoed across the stonework, revealing gargoyle faces screaming silently. There, staring back across the centuries, was Le Stryge, that strange gothic devil, chin resting in his hands, witnessing, from his vantage point, high above the city, the once stylish boulevards succumbing to the slap of African feet. What had her pastor told her as he threaded rosary beads, slowly, almost sexually, between his fingers, '*and the meek shall inherit the earth...*' 'Yeah, right, that always happens,' she cursed, with a wisp of Gauloise breath.

Striking another match she passed like a phantom under the trees on Quai de Montebello. Party people sauntered along the Pont de L'Archeveche, spidery shadows entangling in the wrought iron grills of the bridges and gateways to apartment blocks owned by sell-outs. In the distance, she could hear someone strumming a guitar, a flat voice singing '*Tout les garcons et les filles.*' Such songs were hardly heard now. More often than not it was the reedy sound of pan-pipes or the lazy bang of a steel drum. She dodged past a group of jazz fans heading home, overtaking a staggering drunk weaving wildly across the pavement. It was like the last days of the Roman Empire, people trying to drink themselves into oblivion rather than face the cold hard truth. A whole generation of people in denial. Minority status in their own home and an aggressive neighbour breaking down their door. Some twenty metres behind, the young man with the pony tail, who had followed her from Saint-Michel, reached inside his long coat, fingers wrapping around the handle of a nine millimetre Uzi sub machine pistol.

About one hundred metres beyond the Crypte Memorial, walking parallel on the other bank, she recognised the same middle-aged couple who had been grumbling on the metro escalator as they climbed out of a yellow taxi. The man was speaking rapidly into a mobile phone. His wife was searching for something in her handbag. There was a glint of neon on graphite. For a second she thought it was just a coincidence but then a few strides on she flicked a butt into the gutter and stole a look behind. There was her stalker in the flapping coat. Another man was walking parallel to her on the other side of the road.

'Fucking English,' she murmured to herself.

The right thing to do now was to cut back across the quai and go down Rue de Bernardins, past the shops, which were closed but brightly lit, hook up with some late-nighters in Saint-Germain, and try to lose her tail before getting a lift from some guy out of the centre. But alcohol had somewhat dampened her mind. The feeling of being watched travelled like clammy hands all over her body. Just ahead, a young courting couple embraced against a wall. The man was tall and well built. His muscular arms wrapped around the diminutive brunette. The girl, who seemed reluctant to return his tongue, was slim and pale. Only—her eyes were on the *Pétroleuse*, oblivious to her lover's attentions. Just for a moment the girl's gaze slipped away, her mouth dropped open in an involuntary gesture, reacting to something, but certainly not the man making love to her. Out of the corner of her eye their target saw the man tracking her along the boulevard come out of the shadows, the single beam from a passing Vespa's headlight revealing the wire travelling from under a raised collar up to his ear.

Caged Tiger

The side street where they finally cornered her was still asleep as Lieutenant Bruyere flicked on the headlights and his boss, Inspecteur Fouvier, got in, handcuffed to the girl. No one came to the window to witness the young woman being grappled to the floor. No one took more than a cursory interest in the shouting and the echo of automatics being locked and loaded. Dogs barked as the driver pulled off, his car circling slowly around Fouvier's snatch-squad, who was being de-briefed by his erstwhile wife in her *le manteau naturel fourrure*. The team tidied up the scene and tucked away their weapons as Bruyere made off with the captive.

'Hurry!' said Fouvier.

He wished to avoid the Zouave patrols and felt claustrophobic inside the car. The girl sat in silence, seemingly mesmerised by the beams of the un-marked Peugeot slashing the buildings, angling piss trails of light over Hotel De Ville. Fouvier worried about a sudden intercept. She had friends everywhere. And despite having the state apparatus against them, the resistance had pulled off high profile escapes. They all listened to the 207's engine purr, as army trucks deposited bearded zealots with black flags along with Europol troopers throughout the city.

'Why this way?' asked Fouvier.

'Traffic is bad.' The captive stared at the driver's head as they rolled over cobbles on Île de la Cité. Abyssinian beggars were on the prowl. A clique of transsexuals hovered in a doorway looking for trade. Above the Sainte Chapelle, a slice of lemon moon shone in the night.

'Get Levangie on the phone', Fouvier ordered, 'tell him we've got good news for the Minister.'

Seconds later, Levangie's voice rang out in the car.

'You got her?' he asked excitedly.

'Our British friend swears it's her', replied Fouvier.

'So much for Winston Churchill, what do you say?'

Fouvier looked into the blank face next to him.

'I think we've saved Ben Hassi's testicles!'

The Head of the Security Service laughed with relief. 'Run the usual tests. I must be sure before I tell the Minister anything that may impact on his *couilles*.'

When they stopped the car, Bruyere opened the rear door and yanked the girl out onto the tarmac. He was a well-built man with solid shoulders and a karate black belt. His trainer had always insisted that given a fair chance and a tail wind he could have made the national team. Fouvier looked on, scrutinising the girl, trying to get under her sphynx-like shell.

'Sebastien,' he interrupted, I know you enjoy your work but please be careful with our cargo.' Bruyere nodded, but was thinking of his cousin who had been knee-capped by the resistance for helping a family of newly arrived Muslims evict a French family in Nantes.

'Sometimes my enthusiasm gets the better of me', he said.

'All the same,' said his commander,' there is a time and a place.'

Bruyere lifted her with both hands. 'Sorry, Captain.'

Fouvier opened the palm of his hand to show their prisoner a small purple vial he had rifled from her coat as they had travelled side by side.

'There will be no suicides on my watch,' he informed her. 'You people must be more careful what you have sewn into your clothes.'

'Pig,' she said, spitting into the Inspecteur's face.

Bruyere's instantaneous reaction was to slap her hard around the head. There was a trickle of blood from the corner of the girl's mouth.

'Sorry baby, did I split your lip?'

She glared. '*Connard!*'

In that instant both men could see the caged tiger behind the eyes. Bruyere smiled nervously, imagining ripping claws stretching out for his face.

'*Je t'aime aussi!*' he sang in a high octave.

*

Later, as the cell door crashed behind her, she stood leaning back against the lock mechanism for a few minutes and lit a cigarette. What faced her was a small block room. On the bed, two blankets, a single grey pillow, and a sidelight. To her left was a chipped white basin with no plug, a lime towel and a caustic-looking bar of soap. There was a strong smell of disinfectant. Whitewashed walls stared back at her whitewashed face.

She yawned, slipped off the coat she had been given by her new acquaintance earlier in the evening and threw it on the bed. Six fluid strides and she was looking out of the narrow window into a moon-lit courtyard where cars came and went. Dawn was a long way off. Stubbing a cigarette on the window sill, she wondered who else had been picked up. How many of her comrades may have been 'disappeared'? When would Luc come for her? At irregular intervals a guard's footsteps would echo in the corridor outside and the spy hole in her door would slide open, allowing a glint of light to finger the darkness. The watcher could see her laying back on the bunk, hands behind her head, cigarette in mouth, looking directly back at him.

Around seven o'clock, she began to hear the distant sound of doors clanging and men being roused, coughing and complaining before heading for the showers. The girl guessed she was in the station's isolation cell, reserved for Category A prisoners—hard-core enemies of the government. She ran broken nails through her dark trailing hair in the manner so familiar to her friends.

'So, they have you,' she murmured to herself, 'the bastards!' She lit another cigarette—her last—felt the lurch of an empty stomach complaining at the tobacco abuse, but swallowed hard on the smoke and tried to ignore her hangover. Indulging herself for a moment she looked down at stockinged toes tangoing coquettishly outside the coarse woollen blanket. Smiling, she remembered her shoes at the club in Saint-Lazare and the few hours she had spent with the intriguing Englishman before her arrest. 'I'll kill him before this is over!' she promised herself. Then, even more ominously, she recited breathlessly, 'We are Charles the Hammer's new phalanx, his second coming, a revolutionary vanguard, more determined, better trained, utterly resilient.'

*

Sabine had left Commander Costello with a bad hangover and a worse conscience. He had realised she had given him the slip easily and excused his mistake because of the alcohol and the girl's sexual attraction. Knowing that Fouvier, acting on his tip-off, had taken Sabine into custody had made him uneasy. Professional pride aside, he felt this *La Pétroleuse* represented something elemental.

'I'm a Judas!' he said to himself as he wandered past police check points, looking for a place to eat. The day was cold and grey. Working people pushed by in their long coats and scarves, the detritus of Damascus driving around in unmarked cars. A hand painted sign caught his eye and he stepped past a smoking waitress into a small cafe. Taking a seat he watched as a battered old Citroen van dropped off three boxes of fresh pastries. Eventually the peroxide waitress came over and he tried to place his order in a splutter of Franglais. In the end he was forced to point at the pictures on the plastic menu card. Then the girl tore off a ticket and slid it under a dirty ashtray.

Costello could see the outline of a bra through her cotton blouse. His eyes were drawn to the imitation gold around her neck and the chain circling her bruised ankle as she strutted her feckless backside *en route* for the kitchen. As she pushed on the swing door a thin African torso came into view through the steam. A few market stall traders wandered in swearing about an incident on the roadside. One of them, a young Arab, was holding a blaring radio and when he saw Costello he smiled, showing gold-capped teeth sparkling with saliva. He looked predatory, like a crocodile feeding. Then, kissing the waitress full on the mouth he waved in exultation, as if he had something the customer wanted but could never have. Just for a second Costello remembered Meursault's handgun and the use he put it to on the beach in Camus' *L'Étranger*. The sullen waitress, fresh from her tryst, brought him out of his reverie by throwing a tepid coffee and a chipped plate of burnt croissants down onto the table.

He ate, buttery fingers dripping over the formica table top. Having sobered up a little, he lit a cigarette and stretched his legs. Costello had always been under the impression that fat people lived in America, polite people lived in England, and that Bohemians lived in Paris, but after the last few weeks all his preconceived notions were as dead as the butts in the ashtray before him. The mix of people he had come across here was just the same as in London. The place was a zoo. The policy of prioritising housing for immigrants had transformed the parks and streets, filling the city with threatening physiognomies and the echo of street prayers, straight from Mecca or Medina. Why his own government was covertly supporting the colonisation of France by Third World itinerants remained an issue for him. Surely, the Channel was no great barrier against such a vast, nomadic population. The thousands flooding through the rail tunnel proved that. Or was Prime Minister Miliband, himself elected by a narrow majority, secured only by Muslim-dominated constituencies, just pandering to his newly found allies? Generally, the Parisians were as vacuous a MTV generation as the one at home, opportunistic and fashion obsessed, mesmerised by fads, but without the purchasing power to support their addiction to retail. When he had tried to buy a shirt in the Marais, the shop assistant was rude and uncooperative in line with the Anglophone stereotype of a pretentious Parisian, but otherwise the city had become mongrelised by the modernity that had poisoned the world. Most of the crumbling streets behind the glossy boulevards were filled with the stench of curry and cat pee. It seemed that, instead of frog's legs, couscous was the national dish.

Costello considered the Resistance's case was being made for them. In the *banlieues*, gangs of youths fuelled by crack cocaine took control after sunset and it was common to hear the sound of gunfire well into the night. Often power outages lasted for days in what the government termed urban sensitive zones, as attempts by emergency services to penetrate the dense concrete jungle, with their narrow passageways and high windows, was met by stone throwing and mindless vandalism. Rapes, robbery, and murder went unchecked by the Europol Militia and were openly encouraged by the Caliphate auxiliaries who rumour had it sometimes kidnapped girls off the street for their own gratification. Property theft did not raise an eyebrow, it was so common-place. Whites were openly targeted for mugging by baseball bat-wielding Africans, sauntering in that familiar 'chip on the shoulder' style. Their every glance through malignant chimp-like eyes challenging you to 'disrespect' them so as to have an excuse to attack. Wilding and flash mob sorties were routine, small businesses were struggling, experienced workers were getting laid off because of cheap Chinese imports and soaring commodity prices, even on basic goods. The birth rate among newcomers was swelling like a maternal waistline, oustripping the host population's three to one. It was estimated that the nation would be majority non-white in fifty years. House repossessions were rocketing across the country and even Printemps began to look expensive to bourgeois double income couples. It was no surprise to him that people began to turn elsewhere for answers, to find out how this had happened and who was profiting from the managed chaos that was labelled 21st century France.

How much worse could it get?, he thought to himself. He struck up a fresh cigarette and tried to think about the American beat writers who had hung out in the Rue Git-le-Cœur. Costello had done his homework on the resistance, recognising influences from around the world and across the generations. He recalled one particular piece of research, reading an analysis by Julius Evola on the beatniks, 'in a society, a civilization, like ours, and especially the USA, one must admit that the rebel, the being who does not adapt, the a-social being, is in fact the sanest . . .' *How perceptive*, he concluded, sitting there, sucking on his cigarette. This D'Orlac girl was a set of paradoxes. Modern, certainly; independent and care-free, undoubtedly. A verbal and sexual libertine by all accounts. And yet, after only spending a short time in her company, he sensed an inner dignity that was so lacking in most girls her age. She could have so easily have been just another one of those slack-mouthed slut characters from a Kerouac novel. But this person had a moral certainty and it was that quality that drove her in pursuit of the movement's goals, to save France from destitution and domination by a mud people with a propensity for infinite cruelty.

He had been hoping for something more meaningful from this assignment, perhaps an answer to the psychoanalyst Robert Linder's proposition that a state that strangles life and attacks personality ferments Right-wing anarchism. The fact that Fouvier had called in a favour from his days in Egypt was a ruse. Ten years in counter-terrorism and postings from Serbia to Pakistan had not prepared him for what he faced. This was different. There was something pulling at his heart-strings. For a long time he tried to deny it, but in the end his ancestry got the better of him. These people were fighting to survive. He recalled his father telling him about his own great grandfather's membership of Altiri na hAiséirghe during the Second World War, the bravery of Michael Collins, and of course his Catholic upbringing, first in Wexford and later in Suffolk. Then there was the little issue of attraction. He found this woman challenging and Costello could already gauge that he had a conflict of interest and that did not bode well.

He attempted to distract himself. He remembered buying a dog-eared copy of Françoise Sagan's *L'Arbre voyageur* on a rainy Sunday after his arrival and pulling it out of his jacket pocket he read the first chapter on the metro. There and then he realised Hemingway's *Moveable Feast* had moved. Disillusioned by almost everything except the girl he had pursued and finally cornered the previous night, Costello got up, waited for the hiss of the hydraulic doors opening and stepped onto the drab platform. Almost the first thing he encountered was a gypsy beggar thrusting lavender into his face. He sidestepped the ragged hag and just had enough time to buy another box of smokes before going to the police station.

*

'It's her I tell you,' said Fouvier.

'Are you sure? She looks too normal,' Capitaine Durand of the Sous-Directorate Anti-Terroriste began to reply, just as a third man joined them, staring through a two way mirror into the interrogation room.

'Trust me,' the latest arrival confirmed in an English accent that betrayed Irish origins, 'That is Sabine D'Orlac, *La Pétroleuse.*'

Beyond the glass they could see the same young woman they had picked up off the street the evening before. She was sitting at a table opposite the arresting officer in a black roll neck sweater and dark jeans. In front of her, slightly to the left of her elbow was a blue and yellow Ricard ashtray soiled by two lipstick-smeared butts.

'You've allowed her to wash and change her clothes?' Costello asked.

'We're not the Gestapo!' Fouvier smiled switching on the surveillance intercom between the two rooms.

'Good afternoon,' they heard the policeman say over the speaker as the suspect struggled to make herself comfortable on the hard wooden seat, 'my name is Lieutenant Girard. It is 12.30 pm on the 2nd October.' Then reaching out to adjust the reverb on the recording device, 'We are about to start the interview of Sabine D'Orlac, case number A0165 in the presence of Sergeant Céline Brun', Girard gestured towards a frumpy female colleague standing behind the suspect's chair, her broad back square to the wall, hard mouth curled in disgust. She had looked so much better in her fur coat on Rue de Pontoise the night before. 'You know your rights and obligations as they pertain to your arrest?'

The woman took a deep drag on her cigarette and stared out from under heavy lidded eyes. 'I know people like me have no rights,' she said in a voice that was a stranger to filtered cigarettes.

'Would you care to explain what you mean?'

'Non.' She impertinently exhaled a trail of smoke.

'That remark,' Girard continued, trying to ignore her contempt, 'Are you claiming you have not received due process?'

'I am simply stating that I was kidnapped off the street and brought here against my will,' Sabine said impatiently. She was smoking like she meant business, systematically filling the ashtray before her. When she spoke she kept her body very still but her hands were animated, causing the dark drainpipe trousers to be covered with specks which she carelessly brushed away before settling back behind a fog of cigarette smoke.

'She's making a fool of Girard,' Durand commented bitterly in the adjacent room, 'Fouvier, can't you train your people?'

The Inspecteur ignored the slight, such rivalry between the services was now endemic, indeed encouraged, in Paris' casbah-style politics.

'But you've got to admit she's a good-looking woman,' Fouvier replied wistfully after a moment.

'Not for long. Can you imagine her teeth in a few years time after smoking like that?' Durand was agitated. He wanted to take control of the operation and was under pressure to hand the case over to his colleagues from Ankara and Benghazi.

'It's not her teeth I'd be interested in,' Fouvier laughed. Durand was turning increasingly angry.

'Please confirm your name and your date of birth,' Girard continued mechanically.

'I will not answer your stupid questions,' they heard her say over the relay system. 'You are collaborators and will one day have to answer for your crimes.'

'I swear to God I'm going to slap her dirty mouth!' Durand barked. He got up off his chair and was pacing back and forth.

'Calm down,' Fouvier said, in ushered tones.

'Calm down? Don't you know what that bitch has done?' yelled Durand. He pulled a SP2022 from his shoulder holster. 'I'm going to scare her a bit', he said, walking towards the door. The Englishman stood in his way.

'You'll do nothing of the sort,' he said firmly, signalling for Durand to go back to his seat.

'So you have a few drinks with her and now you're in love?' Durand quipped disdainfully. He went to barge past but before he could force his way through he was quickly folded into a rigid arm-lock, his struggling legs toppling chairs as he was lifted forcibly backwards and wrestled roughly up against the mirror from where his toad-like eyes could see the girl.

'Bastard English,' Durand breathed into the cold hard surface flattening the side of his face.

'Gentle with him, John', Fouvier admonished, 'honestly, you are worse than Bruyere.' The man from the British Special Forces wrenched Durand's wrist backwards, trained fingers pushing down hard on the Parisian's pressure points, forcing the pistol to clang loudly on the ground.

*

'Well now we've got a positive ID what do we do?' Bruyere asked in the quiet of the office. 'Can we hand her over to Durand and his new friends? I don't think we'll get her to talk, she's a hard bitch!'

'She'll crack eventually,' Fouvier guessed, 'but not easily, we've been here three days already and it is only the swab test that's got us anywhere.'

Costello, who had been sitting quietly listening to the Frenchmen's conversation, bent forward, his jaw coming down gently to rest on his upturned fingers.

'I don't think water-boarding is the appropriate method, my friends, not for this one. Drugs, beatings, and sleep deprivation, all have their advantages, but this girl is a special case. There is a key to this woman and if we find it I suspect we will have opened up Pandora's box.'

'That's poetic for a graduate from Hereford,' Fouvier said admiringly.

'Hereford?' Bruyere looked on perplexed.

'The Special Air Services' training centre', Costello explained; 'It's on the English and Welsh border.'

'Rugby!' Bruyere nodded.

'And killing!' Fouvier informed his colleague, slapping him firmly across his broad back.

The three of them had been at Durand's holding centre for thirty six hours now, sending out for food, red wine and cigarettes while they continued questioning the detainee. There were many such clandestine centres dotted around the major cities and larger towns. Originally called 're-adjustment centres for the culturally insensitive,' they had mutated into more formal prisons for political dissidents, persons who did not fear the social ostracism of being called a racist, and therefore required sequestration. Outside, in the small courtyard they could hear the beatings being conducted on patriotic miscreants rounded up after sweeps through the city. The three of them had barely shaved or washed. In fact their prisoner looked in better shape than them. At least she insisted on maintaining her personal hygiene. Instructions to lock-down intel on her arrest had been agreed between the various competing services. The idea was to force co-conspirators like Bodine or Bellew into a rash act or—even better—begin to sweat on the fact she might have talked.

One afternoon, Ben Hassi emerged from his prayer room to attend a de-brief session and asked to meet *La Pétroleuse* in person. They led him down a long corridor to her containment area. Fouvier had taken the precaution to truss Sabine up like Hannibal Lecter, unsure of how the sight of such a profound enemy would excite her. As it turned out Sabine had second-guessed them, anticipating they were intending to show off their prize to someone in authority and though profoundly incensed by the visit, she had decided to meet the offense with - smouldering humour.

'What do you think this is, a freak show?' She declaimed to the Minister's face. 'Now you've seen me you can start swimming home!'

'I can't swim,' Ben Hassi told her.

'So much the better, you can drown and save me a bullet.'

*

Over the next few hours, as Ben Hassi's car drove in convoy down Rue Beaubourg, a number of resistance 'happenings' were kicking off all around the city. Some were light-hearted egg throwing events, like the young brigands who showered the Justice Minister's diplomatic limousine with broken shells as it slowed to take the corner into Rue Chapon, while others involved angry clashes. The Revolutionary Council had already met and been told about Sabine's internment. Luc Dubois was agitating for a full out assault on Durand's facility but both Bodine and Bellew used their cooler, more tactical heads, preferring to take a senior government minister hostage and to try and force an exchange.

'It will demonstrate the equivalence we attach to one of them and one of our own,' Bellew said.

'It will also send a message of commitment to all our political soldiers in captivity', Bodine butted in.

'Either way', Luc shouted, 'let's do it!'

As if on cue, a division of the hated Europol militia were despatched with a few hundred policemen in order to mediate the situation in the streets with their long rubber truncheons and side arms drawn. Governmental aids had got quickly to decision-makers' insisting that the militant student protestors who were wandering up and down Rue du Temple in support of *La Pétroleuse* with their Lambda banners unfurled, chanting their catchphrases 'Defendons nos couleurs!' had to be confronted, lest they gather even more public support.

Within thirty minutes, requisitioned Noctambuses pulled up on the Rambuteau full of loyal Aadils and Aamiras ready to counter demonstrate in support of the government. Men and girls in PLO scarves, grouped under Abd el-Kader flags chanted 'Open minds are colour blind!' from the steps of the Musée Carnavalet. Dogs were turned loose on the native militants, sending them running down the Rue Pavée. They spread out around Rue de Jarente, being picked up in the side streets, alley ways and courtyards near Rue d'Ormesson. Several were knocked down in the stampede and mauled by the police dogs. Occasional gunshots rang out among the apartment blocks, leaving some of the four-legged hunters dead on the street.

Charles Ackmann's Trans Global News Media, which ran a covert cartel with Al Arabiya, began constructing their own fictions about the night's events under a predictable headline:

NEVER AGAIN . . .

First the fascists spat, then they charged, pulling out knives and bats. Surrounding our police, the defenders of public peace, the mob wounded two married officers, the loving fathers of four beautiful French children . . .

The article was accompanied by colour photos of Sergeant Bao Nguyen and Private Idowu Tokuabo with their wives and families in the familiar hairbrushed domesticity that was intended to warm the hearts of the reading public.

*

'You know,' Bruyere said to the other two investigators, genuinely discomfited by the digital files on the laptop in front of him, 'I've been working in the political section for three years and I still don't get these people.'

'I've explained this to you Sebastian!' Fouvier sounded exasperated. 'If you think in terms of the old Right-Left paradigms you will never understand.' He stood up to stretch his legs and went over to the water cooler in the corner of the small crowded office they had commandeered from the still bruised and furious Durand. 'There is as much Ezra Pound as Benito Mussolini in these people's philosophy. They mix everything from Bourbon Catholicism to Maoism.'

'I like it when it's simple: Hitler versus Stalin!'

'The world's moved on I'm afraid', Costello chipped in, 'these types take the best from everywhere and call it integral traditionalism.'

'There you go again—more definitions.'

'Well these guys are a new graft on an old vine,' said Fouvier.

Bruyere threw up his hands. 'Look, some of the key ideologues of traditionalist thinking are people like René Guenon. They are not an aberration. The resistance's form of traditionalism isn't simply nostalgic, it is spiritual and eternal.'

'But it's still them and us, right?' said Bruyere.

'I think it's us versus us this time', Costello murmured, as much for his own benefit as Bruyere's.

'Just like 40-45!' Fouvier added sipping from the wax cup.

Bruyere shrugged, 'You are losing me again.'

Costello tried to help. 'Well, for example, people like Arnaud Bellew argue that for decades after the last war the French state has brainwashed the population into recoiling from the image of Petain and deny that there was any good under Vichy. They might say that in October '45 the liberated Free French had metaphorically exorcised its demons by tying Pierre Laval to a wooden post in Fresnes Prison and shooting him dead for his ideals.'

'He was a traitor!' Bruyere insisted.

'*Vive la France!*' Fouvier inserted.

'Thousands of Frenchmen shouted *murderers* at his executioners from behind iron bars,' continued Costello. 'A hundred thousand alone were killed in the post-liberation orgy of vengeance; as many as a million interned; hundreds of thousands sentenced to hard labour; a further quarter of a million deprived of their basic civil rights and hundreds upon hundreds driven into exile overseas. The intellectuals, philosophers, and historians amongst the resistance will vary on many points but their general consensus is that, ever since '45, plebiscite after plebiscite has returned socialist, former communist, liberal, or conservative politicians to the Elysées

Palace. All of whom have a tacit agreement or private understanding among themselves, a sort of post-war coalition of conformity, beholden as they were and still are to supra-national interests. Presidents like Mitterand, Sarkozy, and Hollande these resistants think of as maggots wriggling about inside a putrefying body politic in an ever-advancing state of decay. You see, for the thinkers behind this movement *they* are the real collaborators, tools of free-market financial and multinational manipulators, little stuffed puppets dancing to the intellectual string-pulling of faddist existentialists like Sartre, Lacan, and their disciples. They despise this new civic religion, this egalitarian, politically correct certainty liberals and socialists have in their own moral rectitude.'

'But the world's moved on!' said Bruyere.

'And that's the issue for them. They think we've moved in the wrong direction.'

'But they can't turn the clock back!'

'They don't want to. They want to take the clock off the wall and re-design the mechanism.'

Fouvier became animated as he walked back with his drink, listening to Bruyere's and Costello's banter. He said, 'France has changed. Some say for the worst. This is not the France I was born into and certainly not the France of my parents. It does not look or even smell the same!'

'Things change!' said Bruyere.

'Yes, one of the Resistance's gurus, Arthur Moeller van der Bruck, said traditionalists have no ambition *to see the world as a museum*, their concern is for *what is* and *what will be*,' Fouvier answered.

'Sticking it to the world!' Bruyere shouted.

'Giving modernity the finger!' Costello joked.

'Crazy, can't be done,' Bruyere could not be won over.

Costello turned serious for a moment, 'Is it any more crazy than living in a land where the countryside is being deliberately depopulated and the cities filled up with foreigners? Jobless itinerants and struggling students compete for low paid jobs and living space in all the overcrowded urban areas?' He winked. 'Where undercover cops slip into trendy clothes and infiltrate protest movements? Some even sell hashish openly on the street in the safe knowledge that stage-managed arrests and theatrical beatings are a cover for them to pass on their messages.'

Fouvier slipped back into his seat opposite the bewildered Bruyere and continued the litany with deliberation.

'Where the universities, the bureaucracy and the media have derided self-reliance, discipline, and patriotic feelings for generations and imported a disabling lifestyle filled with consumerism and narcissism? Where divide and conquer is the objective? Where multiculturalism, sexual liberation, and the welfare bribe can keep people ineffective, decadent, and compliant just long enough so that their self-appointed masters can replace them with immigrants who in turn can take their land and their jobs from right under their noses? It has worked before in other countries, why not here in the heart of Europe? After all, that is what the Barcelona Agreement is all about. You could say they have paved the way for the Eurabic Accords.'

'But these big meetings and their grand announcements don't really change day-to-day life for the average Jean and Céleste on the street?' Bruyere had began to sound angry.

'You don't think so?' Fouvier was on the edge of his seat.

Bruyere was insensed. 'Christ, you are beginning to sound sympathetic to them.'

'And why wouldn't anyone be?' put in Costello. 'With unrestricted movement of people between the Muslim world and France guaranteed by right to both peoples? When all Muslims, including French converts, are subject to Shari'ah law and the judgements of Shari'ah courts only regardless of geography? Where Muslims have the unrestricted right to worship in the workplace, the public realm and the mosque as they see fit and Christians should be respectful of Muslim communities when they display so-called crusader symbols like the holy crucifix? Then there's the small matter of the demolition of our churches and the free conduct of hymn and prayer.'

'No one is Christian anymore, anyway!' Bruyere laughed. 'Who cares?'

'You or your children might,' Fouvier muttered. 'When an agreed quota system in employment regulation discriminates against you because an employer fails to meet the current minimum number of ethnics in his workforce. Or when by public statute and planning permission all villages, towns, and cities should have available Halal retailers so that the few remaining French-owned stores and supermarkets must offer Halal products or face the threat of sanctions. For God's sake, last year they even tried to bring in a Jizya tax on Christians!'

'That seems unlikely.'

'Unlikely?' Fouvier guffawed sarcastically. 'It is happening, only the media is banned from reporting too fully on issues like female circumcision, honour killings, or arranged marriages in the interests of social cohesion. These people want homosexual acts between men made illegal but permissible, providing they repudiate their sin, whilst homosexual acts between women should they argue lead to encasement or public stoning!'

PART TWO

Two Years Earlier

Sabine paused over the washbasin, allowing the cold water to flow delicately through her fingers. Beyond the open window she could see wisteria climbing white walls and hear the sound of children playing in the yard below. In the mirror before her the reflection of a sallow-faced young man with a bronze 'Reyn til Runa' badge pinned to his overcoat's lapel leered over her pink, round shoulder. His warm hands cupped her naked breasts.

She had first noticed Luc sitting alone amongst the café tables at Centre Georges Pompidou. His expressive eyes had devoured her has she read a copy of *Le Figaro*, smoking Gitanes over an espresso. Later Sabine saw him again and, taking pity on what she took at first to be a shy boy, she invited her admirer to sit down. Sabine's initial impression was mildly sceptical. He was pale, slim-framed. What at first she took to be Luc's natural sensitivity she soon came to realise was limited only to intimacy with girls. They went to a Futurist art exhibition together where he spoke effusively about the paintings of Giorgio Morandi and Gino Severini, dined together over an open copy of Marinetti's manifesto and she listened while he told her about his love of Wyndam Lewis. She thought he was one of those typical young would-be philosophiles, long faced, hands waving, cigarette jabbing like a sword from behind a café table covered in half-drained wine glasses. Later she became entranced and began to learn from him. His interests were eclectic and he floated like a butterfly between flowers, touching on various topics that she was unfamiliar with. Luc would say things like 'I know progress is good, but it's killing us. The world is getting too small and mass media too powerful and too big.'

*

Spring and Early Summer Statutes:

12th March. The Geneva Protocols are confirmed, beginning the legal process of multiple citizenships for all inhabitants of nation-states bordering the Mediterranean.

29th May. The French National Assembly introduces formal quotas for the representation of Partner States from North Africa in all its ministries, committees and security council meetings.

3rd July. Treaties are signed with Côte d'Ivoire, Senegal, Burundi, and Nigeria for unrestricted access for migrant workers in the fields of green technologies, computer science and bio-diagnostics to fill skill shortages in these key French industries.

*

Luc and Sabine would meet next to where the coffee-thick Seine ebbed and flowed under Pont Lazare and walk for hours under a heavy sky bruising for rain. Soon, without realising it, they were holding hands, running between the traffic, heading for the Louvre. They spent the whole afternoon trailing through the long corridors crammed full of renaissance art and Rodin's sculptures. Later, half famished, he took her to eat Italian and then on to a little bar he frequented with his university friends. They climbed up on red swivel chairs under a large painting of the blue mosque in Istanbul, talking through the night.

On one occasion, about six in the morning, just after saying *au revoir* to her new friend, Sabine made straight for home. She knew this meant a predictable fight with Edouard over coffee and chocolatines, but she had nowhere else to go. After being forced to leave Le Mans Sabine had taken up with Edouard, an itinerant painter, and they sort of fell into a mutually convenient co-dependency. She had begun to resent it recently, but was not sure if that was because of the growing sexual boredom or an increasing confidence in her own abilities to fend for herself. While walking across Mitterand's alienating brave new world of open plazas towards the railway station in Montparnasse, she had noticed her stockings had laddered and stopped to remove them. The flash of black suspenders even at that ungodly hour drew a response from the Pakistani workmen standing high above her on the steel balustrades caging La Coupole. They whistled at her and made all sorts of big promises that no mortal man could hope to deliver.

This was still a time of relative economic success before the first wave of big bank crashes. Commuters began pouring out of a nearby concrete ant hill ahead, suburbanite blank faces seemingly chained to the black leather briefcases swinging at their sides, oblivious to the biological time bomb ticking away in their midst, these free-marketers of and princes of the bloated public sector pretending to themselves that turning France into an illegitimate son of Africa would not change their comfortable lives or the future safety of their children. Hundreds and hundreds of shoes stepping all around, trying desperately not to make eye contact with Sabine as she called back to the men hanging off the scaffolding above them. It seemed to her that the spirit of Jean Cocteau had long since departed the Fourteenth Arrondissement. Now, the latest laptops and mobiles were everyone's badges of success.

'Pigs!' she snorted at the bespectacled businessmen, 'Go run to your pathetic little office jobs!'

Just for a moment she wondered how many would later take their bimbo doll-like secretaries off to some seedy hotel for post-lunch sex. Walking on, the Tour Montparnasse loomed overhead like an inquisitive giant, watching her every move. She passed the Maison des Artistes, where Edouard was a member. She could not remember how many times he had dragged her in to read newsletters and talk to his arty friends. She stopped by a large billboard advertising an American Film Season. She was checking out the schedule and prices when her eyes were irresistibly drawn to the left of the box office by a life-sized doll in a G-string. Sabine could not help but think how it resembled one of her best friends, hanging up there in the window advertising 'A Hot Lesbian Bed Show.' There was a sign stuck to the glass, letters scrawled in Arabic. Such shops, it seemed, were still licensed as part of the Eurabic ethos of *cultural understanding*. So were the working girls, who were already beginning to congregate at either end of La Rue de la Gaite under the supervision of their Albanian pimps. It was noticeable that most of the women were fair or red haired, though some black booty was also available. But no middle-eastern beauties: they were consciously preserved and protected. A tumble-faced old hippy with long greasy hair was rolling a suspicious-looking cigarette in the litter strewn doorway of L'Odyssex. The stench of soiled clothing filled the air. She could see his trousers were soiled with faeces.

Sabine decided to keep moving. She was cold and footsore and her head throbbed like a wailing police siren. It was nearly 8 a.m. when she eventually came in sight of her flat. The shutters were closed. This did not surprise her. She knew from bitter experience how Edouard worked through the night. He loved to paint in the dark. Sometimes he would never come to bed. Sabine used the key as silently as she could and made for the staircase. Her finger hit the light switch, but the bulb had blown. Her eyes spotted a shadowy shape rubbing against her legs. Beckett leapt up with a hiss, his hair standing to attention down the full length of his long sleek back.

'Shush, stupid cat!' she hissed. The green-eyed moggy curled around her feet as she began to mount the stairs, step by step, flight by flight, circling up to the attic. The whole house was quiet. No one stirred. The cat was mewling for milk so she sat down on the bottom step of the very last rise and reached out a hand. It was a chance to draw breath before the inevitable scene. As she sat there running her fingers through Beckett's coat she thought how different it might have all been. She remembered going to the riverside with Edouard to watch the barges as they floated by in the clear spring sunshine. Their glimmering paintwork echoing like the pale summer ghosts of Rimbaud's rhymes across the water.

No sound came from the room above. He could be lying comatose up there, surrounded by dirty needles. She reached into her purse and found a coin. 'Heads I go, tails I stay,' she said quietly to herself. The coin came up heads and she rose to go. But the door creaked open and she was bathed in the orange glow of their hall light.

'Sabine, is that you?' Edouard was on the landing. She looked up to see his hairy chest staring at her with a spiteful macho expression. 'Where the hell have you been?'

'Nowhere special, and don't shout, I've got an awful head!' By the third step she was already wondering why he had not stayed there on the landing readying himself to hit her. The usual scenario was to slap her face with the back of his hand before she started to throw things. Right from the top of her head to the tips of her toes she was aware of a break in this ritual. From the moment Sabine swung open the door she could smell it: woman. Edouard was over by the window holding a large cup of breakfast coffee and there, chain-smoking on top of their duvet, was her best friend in the city, Anneke, lying splay-legged, displaying her snatch like an open jar of wet liver.

*

She moved out that very day, calling Luc on his mobile. Within a few weeks they had become lovers and taken a cramped, book-filled Left Bank attic apartment overlooking the river. It was a room with a narrow iron bed, a small musty *en suite*, rickety table, and two wooden chairs. For Sabine it was an opportunity to play house, somewhere to lose herself in the dream of the family life she had never really had. On summer evenings she would stand in her underwear on the narrow balcony and cast burnt out stubs into the Seine. For Luc it was a source of pure enchantment and mystery. He had never lived with a woman before. He felt cosseted in an atmosphere of decadence. He was fascinated by all Sabine's personal effects. The sponge in the shower, sanitary towels, even a stocking draped over the back of the chair took on voluptuous aspects. The very walls seemed impregnated with the intimacy of their lovemaking and the comfort of warm cotton sheets.

*

Late Summer and Autumn Statutes:

1st August. Race Reparation Tribunals commence—over 200 officers are charged with having made ethnically motivated arrests—minimum compensation packages for the victims of such police brutality are set at three hundred thousand Euros.

22nd September. The Committee of Civil Commissioners agrees amnesty for all immigrant prisoners regardless of the severity of their crime due to inherent racism of the French Judiciary prior to 2015.

2nd October. The Sanctuary Cities of Southern France formerly adopt a policy of positively managing out the teaching of French History in favour of curricula that better reflects the national and racial composition of the new student demographic.

*

Once when Luc came back after a night out with his friends he found her in their room at the top of the stairs. Their narrow bed was in the corner, a single bulb dangling from the ceiling. The gas fire hissed. The tang of cigarette smoke hung in the air. Sabine was leaning on the mantle-piece, one hand trailing, the other resting on her hip. She had taken off her dress and cast it on the floor. One strap of her cotton top slipped down over her shoulder as she raised her head when Luc came in. Sabine ran a hand through her hair.

'You're late. You're food is cold', she laughed.

'What did you cook?'

Sabine smarted, frowned, and shook her head determined to carry on the pretence. 'Your favourite, of course!'

She stepped forward unhooking the remaining strap, letting the top cascade over her breasts. Luc watched her walk about the room in front of him, her thumbs sliding under elasticated knickers, easing them over her hips.

'Nice,' Luc breathed. Sabine stood in front of him, legs apart, the triangular mound of pubis thrusting towards his face. When he reached out to touch her she turned on him quickly. Sabine's lips were open for love, her eyes shone with wantonness.

Luc killed the light with one flick of the switch. He felt her trembling. Gradually his eyes could make out the dim shapes of furniture gathering around to witness their mad midnight ramblings. She clung on to him, holding his arms tight and wrapping her legs around his body. Luc licked her eyelids until they opened up to him and then he ran his tongue down her throat. When he made to penetrate her Sabine drew away. Cautiously he tried again, mentally working out her menstrual cycle. Afterwards she sat on the edge of the bed, crouched and tense, staring up into the moonlight like a frightened animal listening for a predator, sprung ready for danger.

'I don't know what the problem is,' she whispered.

'Relax!'

Luc raised himself on one elbow and fondled a cooling breast. He pressed a kiss to her nape and watched the fair skin's reflex as the sensation travelled all the way up to her hairline. Sabine's sweat smelled of schoolgirl puberty. The night was perfectly still. Their eyes could just make out the ruby twinkle of an airplane's ground light through the attic window.

The Prophet

arly on weekend mornings he would steal a car and drive her out of the city to escape the plague of Roma pickpockets flooding the Champs-Élysées. Beyond the drab, decaying suburbs they travelled along clear roads lined with trees, like Napoleon's troops marching towards the horizon.

He was driving fast to impress her with his skill.

'You know who I feel like?' he asked her.

'No, who?'

'Roger Nimier!'

'Who's that?'

Luc grinned malevolently. 'A writer who drove his Aston Martin off a bridge in La Celle-Saint-Cloud. He was doing over one hundred and fifty per hour.'

Sabine frowned. 'Never heard of him!'

'I'm not surprised,' Luc confirmed, 'Nimier was one of the Hussards, like Antoine Blondin. He wrote *The Swords* and *The Blue Hussar* and opposed the existentialist Left clique. That's the reason you never hear of him.'

Sabine shrugged an acknowledgement that she wanted him to explain what he meant.

'Well, you see, those Left-leaning literary arse-kissers came to be the cultural orthodoxy after the last war. They despised film, art, and literary critics like Maurice Bardèche for example. Men of talent and distinction who had no option but to set up their own publishing houses like *Les Sept Couleurs* because they were excluded from the mainstream for their sacrilegious alternative views. The Left's high priest, André Malraux, even became a Minister of Culture and authors like Nimier and traditional-ist-leaning philosophers, like Chardonne and Morand, were consigned to oblivion for being heretics.'

For the next fifty kilometres Luc edified her reciting snatches from Alain-Fournier's *Le Grand Meaulnes* and Henry de Montherlant's *Songe*. She forgave his vanity, amazed at his ability to recall whole sections from the books without faltering once. Grating through the gears at a junction just outside Laval, he turned to Sabine and asked if she had ever read Orwell's *1984*.

'Non,' she shook her head, 'What's it about?'

Luc sighed.

'Newspeak, thought crime, Big Brother . . . in other words everything you think you know, or have ever been taught!'

'What do you mean?'

'I mean we're being constantly lied to.'

'How?'

'Well, for example, did you know that there are thousands of letters from people like the wife of the Mayor of Caen complaining about how the British and the Americans behaved during the Second World War?'

'Non!'

'Yeah, and I bet you didn't know that seventy seven thousand French civilians were incinerated by Allied air raids between 1941 and 1944, that the militants of the Breton Gwenn ha Du and Breiz Atao fought on alongside the Wehrmacht at Lorient, Saint-Nazaire and Brest long after the fall of Berlin? Or that 350,000 so called collaborators were arrested and thrown into concentration camps after the liberation, or that milkmaids in Normandy had to go about their work under armed guard because of the number of rapes committed by American ancillaries?'

Sabine's face was pale.

'Even my great grandmother was forced out into the square in Champeaux . . .'

'La tonte?'

'They scraped her head until it bled!'

'Why?'

'Because she sold bread to the enemy.'

'That is terrible.'

'There were over 20,000 women attacked like that and God knows how many summary executions in orchards and schoolyards by firing squad.'

'You never see it in documentaries', Sabine admitted.

'Well Sartre and de Beauvoir didn't care to mention it. Even today Emgann are maligned as *maquis blanc*. It shows how controlled the supposedly free French press really is!' Luc swung the wheel to take the 164 for Loudeac, 'There is no doubt about it. We live in a subtle but authoritarian liberal state!'

As they drove Sabine lay back enjoying the wind running through her hair and began thinking of her childhood. She had sang *antifone* for Compline in the big cathedral and stood shoulder to shoulder competing with the boys over who could throw stones the furthest across the big car park. She was a tomboy at heart, climbing trees, playing football and lighting matches under frogs. Later all that changed. One day she had gone to the toilet only to find a red splot on the gusset of her knickers and thought she had been shot.

Luc's teenage years were easier for him to recall and talk about. Despite his rebellious nature he was a well-cared-for child and his teachers' report card noted his written work was 'Good,' 'Conscientious,' and 'Imaginative.' When the day's lessons were over, he would often wander home with the other boys. In the privacy of one of the cabal's bedrooms, with the door slammed on adult interference, cigarettes lit, they would talk about girls. At home he often spurned school text books for novels by Hermann Hesse, like *Knulp* and *Steppenwolf,* the very antithesis of the smug, small-minded, and ugly self-interest of the people he witnessed all around him every day. His stubby pencil underlining one sentence in particular 'A wild longing for strong emotions and sensations seethes in me, a rage against the toneless flat, normal and sterile life. I have a mad impulse to smash something, a warehouse perhaps, or a cathedral, or myself, to commit outrages . . .' It was a fateful premonition of his life's future path.

*

He parked the car and they walked arm-in-arm through the narrow harbour streets of Concarneau. Above them gulls circled over the Baie de la Foret, swooping down on rusting trawlers, then rising again, their yellow bills streaming silver-speckled tunny and sardines, which they sometimes spilled back onto the slimy decks. Pink entrails writhed to the rhythm of the wind. Crossing the bridge from the mainland Sabine and Luc passed under the mediaeval arch into Ville Close where great granite walls sheltered them from a wicked westerly rushing in off the sheet metal sea. Bearing to the left as they climbed the worn steps towards Vauban's citadel Sabine noticed Luc was laughing to himself.

'Why do you smile like that all the time?' she asked.

'You will see soon enough' Luc replied.

Hand in hand they mounted the cobbled ramparts of the city, looking out through loopholes cut into the fortress toward the grey sea beyond.

All along Rue Vauban shops bustled with activity. Luc bought roasted chestnuts from a street vendor under the shadow of the old gunpowder tower and they stood together silently on the pavement, hands dipping into the hot packet, watching the ferment of the restaurants and the bars. Girls in traditional Breton costumes came and went carrying bowls of steaming mussels, bottles of white wine cooled on tables covered with vases of freshly cut flowers and blue chequered table clothes. Eventually Luc winked at Sabine, circled her waist with his snaking arm and they progressed along the crowded street towards Musée de la Peche.

'You know', Luc began saying, 'Gauguin got beaten up by a gang of sailors here.'

'Really?'

'Yes, they broke his leg and his Javanese mistress stole everything from his studio and then deserted him.'

'A true artist suffers', Sabine quipped.

'Not like these Americans who play at it', Luc said, pointing to the fish stalls where middle-aged foreigners mimicking bohemians haggled in chewing-gum accents with disgruntled locals. Taking the corner into a stone-edged square they noticed an immediate change of atmosphere. Sabine sensed the tension in the air straight away.

'France Libre, France Libre!' went the chant. A man with a stubbled scholarly beard was standing on a chipped grey statue plinth in a long flapping coat with a megaphone to his mouth. It was Arnaud Bellew. All around him were banners saying *Non a l'unification avec l'Afrique!*

'History,' he bellowed, 'Who's history? Not ours . . .'

'Give us back our respect!' shouted someone from the crowd.

'They've stolen it', retorted the speaker. 'Who learns about us anymore? We are just wreckers and exploiters who grew fat on colonialism!'

'But my father was just a steel worker from Alsace,' screamed a girl somewhere, 'No one gave us anything we didn't work for!'

'Precisely!' came the reply. 'Our forebears dug the coal, built the cathedrals, and cultivated the land from the soil of Verdun to the rooftops of Aix. France is our inheritance by right, it is not theirs to squander.' Luc pulled Sabine deeper into the mass of bodies. The speaker's voice rang out above their heads. 'And who gave them the right anyway? Where does it say the French have given up the will to live?'

'Nowhere!'

'Traitors!' yelled Luc. He felt Sabine's hand slip down inside his trousers.

'Fuck the government!' he heard her shout. Luc smiled.

'That's it,' he encouraged, 'Fuck them all!'

'Fate decrees there are winners and losers, my friends,' said the speaker, 'Our children will judge us by what we do today, tomorrow is too late . . .'

'Boo! Hang the traitors,' chanted the audience. 'La cause du peuple!'

'So comrades, I ask you one simple question, who's turn is it today? Who will win and who will lose?'

'It's our turn,' resounded the voices, 'We will win!'

The crowd pressed in closer around the monument. Luc felt Sabine's breasts drill into his back like nuclear warheads as she clung to him.

'And win we will,' continued the speaker, 'because we have leaders and visionaries on our side.' Then, waving his hand in a contemptuous gesture towards the thin police cordon between himself and the counter-demonstrators huddled together under crimson banners, penned back behind metal railings, 'while they only want to deny who we are and transform us into something we are not and never will be!'

This was almost too much and inflamed raw passions. 'Merde!' came back from the other side. Luc could feel Sabine's warm palm cup his scrotum. Beer bottles were thrown, glass smashing against stone, a red flare danced jerkily across the cobblestones between the opposing groups.

Then an outburst of clapping rolled through the audience and Sabine saw, out of the corner of her eye, a fair blue-eyed man in his early thirties being hoisted onto the shoulders of an advancing cohort. A cheer went up as the procession carried him to the front.

'Laurent! Laurent!' went up the call

'And talking of leaders,' the speaker remarked, 'We have among us a true patriot. Welcome, my friend,' he said, reaching out a hand, 'I can see six months in Sante has not left so much as a mark on you,' he quipped. The makeshift entourage deposited their chisel-jawed hero onto the plinth and the speaker leaned forward offering the megaphone to the new arrival, whose sparkling azure eyes caught the daylight as he turned to greet his folk. Hard fingers ran through corn-blonde hair.

'Thank you comrade,' began Laurent Bardet, raising a clenched fist towards their opponents, 'My probation officers,' he nodded over to the far side of the square, where a group of plain-clothes officers lurked uncomfortably under an elm tree, 'are here to make sure I don't say anything that may incite violence . . .' He smiled mischievously, 'I mean, me, of all people?' There was a peel of laughter.

Then loosening the scarf about his neck and unfastening his jacket, he began. 'You know, I had a lot of time recently to become acquainted with The Bible. That's because it was the only book they allowed me to read!'

'Bastards!' people jeered. Laurent smirked.

'So I'm sorry if I sound like I am giving a sermon but there is one extract which I feel is rather apt and I want to share it with you. It is from Deuteronomy, Chapter 28, and it goes like this . . . "Your sons and your daughters shall be given to another people, while your eyes look on and fail with longing for them all the day; and it shall not be in the power of your hand to prevent it. A nation which you have not known shall eat up the fruit of your ground and all your labours; and you shall be only oppressed and crushed continually; so that you shall be driven mad by the sight your eyes shall see". Laurent's left hand made the sign of the cross. Another ripple of mirth ran through the gathering. Sabine noticed a semi-circle of young men and women amid the demonstrators who wore dark roll-up neck sweaters, leather jackets, and sunglasses.

Now, in the presence of Laurent Bardet, their standard bearer, the momentum changed, every second pulsed and throbbed with a new mystic urgency in the minds of the people listening. His voice began slowly at first, almost sexually arousing the audience. Sabine had Luc's penis in her hand and felt her own labia moisten to the caressing tones coming through the megaphone.

'So what does blood mean to us?' Laurent asked, 'well I will tell you. It means the Seine, the Loire, and the Garonne. It means the sweat of people who have toiled to bring in the harvest, the very juice in our vines . . .'

'French blood!' a man called, saluting vigorously.

'. . . it is the rain that waters our mountains and floods our fields,' Bardet confirmed. 'You know, from the earliest dawn of time we have lived here, suffered here, shed our blood here. Men have fought in battle, women have died in childbirth, so we can be French in our own land.'

'Give us back our country!'

'*Vive la République!*' Laurent called aloud and his frenzied acolytes broke through the police lines, charging towards their enemies gathered under red flags with stones and knives in hand.

The Disciple

She was theirs from the start. It was instinctive and adrenalin-driven. The columns marching under swathes of tricolors being abused and spat upon by placard-waving *Multi-Culti* fanatics nightly on TV caused a counter-reaction. Sabine was there when the clubs were wielded and the police charges broke up the demonstrations, leaving splinter groups to fight running battles in the streets of all major towns in France. At first expressions like 'ethnopluralism' and *'zone d'occupation americaine'* were confusing to her, but after leafing through some Guillaume Faye and Ernst Niekisch her appetite was wetted and she began searching in the piles of books Luc left scattered around the flat while he was in class.

Sitting in her underwear, cigarette in hand, she started turning the pages of well-thumbed works by Georges Dumezil, Ernst Jünger, and Oswald Spengler. Returning home, Luc would find Sabine engrossed in some political or philosophical textbook.

Impressed with her diligence he would lecture her over coffee.

'Like Foucault says', he was fond of beginning, 'for nearly forty or fifty years the only legitimate political discourse was through the twin lens of Marx and Freud. This stranglehold loosened in the transition from the old to the new millennia. No longer are the prophetic words of Louis-Ferdinand Céline, *The more one is hated, I find, the happier one is* only true of our activists and militants. Now that they are the mainstream we are the political dissenters, the outsiders and individuals that Deleuze and Guattari call true individuals in the purest sense', he pushed a copy of *Anti-Oedipus* across the table towards her, 'You see, it is ironic, we are the ones fighting against a unitary, paranoid mono-culture . . . we are the champions of difference over uniformity . . . we are the glamorous ones, now!'

She nodded. The message was clear.

Luc began taking her to party meetings and she helped out at the organisation's office as they attempted to develop a political machine. It was there that she was introduced to the man in the long coat who she had first seen on the plinth in Concarneau. Arnaud Bellew was very welcoming and informal, mixing easily with the young students. Franck Bodine was slightly stiff, which was predictable given his military background. When Sabine saw him for the first time he was issuing hurried orders to resistance activists in the cramped apartment above Rue Racine. They were predominantly clean cut, hair *en brosse* provincials, mixed with pro-Group Union Defense university intellectuals, sitting amongst the banners, photocopying machines, and ink-wet posters, fresh off the printing press.

'The Anglo Saxon model may have defined economic history for the last three hundred years,' they would hear Bellew say, 'but the politics and ideology of France gave birth to the world's revolutions, bringing forth ideas like nationalism, codes of law, a system of technical organisation, and a metric system for measurement.'

When he was in full motivational flow he would usually quote the great French philosophers and thinkers, but on this occasion she remembered him saying something by Joan of Arc and it stuck in her mind: 'One life is all we have and we live it as we believe in living it. But to sacrifice what you are and to live without belief, that is a fate more terrible than dying.'

Sabine was however increasingly drawn to the action-orientated former Legionnaire. For Bodine, De Gaulle was a traitor. He argued compromise can only be considered between equals.

'With hindsight,' he would begin, 'the General's duplicity over Algeria may have been pragmatic, but it cost the lives and property of 400,000 Pied-Noir. How many more now in the heart of France, today? In the 1960's when news broke of the secret negotiations with Ben Bella's FLN at Hotel du Parc in Evian most honourable Frenchmen considered it an insult to the dead of Philippeville. There in that small mining town a ferocious and unprovoked attack on the European settlers by their Muslim neighbours left the nation traumatised. School children had had their brains dashed out against the walls of a kindergarten, women were raped and disembowelled, and the men were nailed Jesus-like to the doors of their homes.' Bodine saw his nation's future in the past. Yet, when only a few decades later the current government signed the 'Open Borders Treaty,' there were few in the homeland who foresaw the consequences. The logic of history was being ignored. The biological clock was ticking. 'No one could deny that the memory of those queuing Pied-Noir families, standing so forlorn on the docks, waiting anxiously in the heat for the passenger ships to come back over the horizon was anything but a French retreat. Once aboard the liners, having cleared the harbour breakwater, the reluctant passengers would drop their luggage and gather at the bow looking back in silence on *Algerie française*. In the distance they could hear the shrieks of the *fellagha* from the city's rooftops and see the hordes charging through the streets, smoking kif, green flags flapping in the breeze. The escapees whispered among themselves 'We are not repatriates, we are refugees, because we are not going to France—we are leaving it'.

Bodine would often use such images as a preamble to his speeches. 'Where can the French go now,' he asked, 'England?' In back street meeting rooms and town squares he would speak out 'Not satisfied with liberation within a generation the Africans' thoughts turned to invasion. If you don't believe it, listen to the words of Abu Imran, one of their spokesmen living in Belgium . . . 'We won't rest until Europe has become an Islamic state. And then we will march on toward the White House and the Vatican . . .' Since the middle sixties Mediterranean sea ports like Marseilles had become the bridgehead from where the invasion had been launched, at first through the womb and now by the sword as the ebb and flow of the demographic tidal wave dictated. Bodine was strenuous when he made this point to an audience. 'The Algeria of our forefathers was a turning point, French civilisation was no longer expanding, it was contracting, and defeat at Dien Bien Phu confirmed bravery and skill could be overcome by the mindless mass.' The logical conclusion was obvious to all. 'In the decades following the surrender of *Algerie Française* the French government has sought to accommodate the population bulge in the developing world by appeasement. This has been achieved by a range of buy-offs in the form of interest-free foreign loans, medical aid by Médecins Sans Frontières and of course, immigration. The latter justified under the guise of labour shortages in the home country, but now they have gone even further through the mechanism of the EU by actively supporting *mondialism* and all its poisonous byproducts.'

After classes they would drink with Luc's student friends in the bars and cafes around the Quartier. On one particular occasion they were joined by some dark-eyed Spanish sympathisers in long black coats who were on a student exchange programme from Madrid. Their leader was a proud descendant of Falangists who had purged the *pueblos* of Communists during the campaign in Granada. They gathered in La Parcheminerie. The restaurant was busy as they sat around a table in a small upstairs room with a low ceiling and an open sash window. Besides themselves there were a few couples spooning oysters and sipping white wine.

The waiter came over, inspected the tablecloth critically and decided to change it. Luc ordered a carafe of *vin rose* and *hors d'œuvres*.

After much chatter and smiles the slim-hipped waiter scribbled down their order and soon returned with *pâté maison* and crusty white bread. The wine was light, dry, and cool.

Their olive-skinned Iberian guests proposed a toast to *El Ausente*, everyone raised their glasses, 'Jose Antonio ¡Presente!' they said respectfully, then, '¡Viva la muerte!'

Over shelled langoustine Luc circulated papers he had worked on during the last two weeks.

'I am recommending we divide the organisation into three main sections,' he said, 'the militant section will be responsible for the mobilisation of the masses, whose purpose would be to get people out to vote, march and defend the streets; the psychological section, to carry out information and propaganda activities and develop the party's doctrine and ideology; and lastly the underground direct action units, to take the battle to our enemies.'

Everyone was enthusiastic.

'I can take it to the next council meeting if everyone is behind me.'

'You should,' said one of their guests in broken French, 'I have seen your city and you have no time to lose!'

There was a lull in the conversation as they cleared their plates and recharged their glasses.

'Would you like me to call for the next course?' Luc asked.

'Do you mind if I have another cigarette first?' Sabine replied.

'Why not?' he shrugged.

Sabine struck a light and leaned back inhaling the smoke deeply.

'What do you think of my programme?' Luc asked her directly, while the others talked amongst themselves.

'Do you want my honest opinion?'

'Of course!'

She sighed. 'It may be too radical for some of the more conservative elements in the leadership.

Later, after a movie, they walked. In less than a hundred metres they were stopped twice and asked to show their papers by Europol militia of Nigerian origin.

'This is what I hate,' said Luc.

Sabine took him by the arm. 'Our time will come . . .'

They drank tea in a small cafe.

Sabine teased him: 'Did you find the girl in the movie seductive?'

'Yes, I suppose so.'

'She had no bosom. Women need curves, otherwise they're sexless!'

He nodded, but thought of imagining her naked later when masturbating. 'The movie was good though, didn't you think?'

Sabine shook her head.

Luc swirled the spoon before asking, 'There have been times tonight when you've seemed very distant, almost unhappy . . .'

Sabine gripped her bag and made to leave, scraping the legs of her chair on the wooden floorboards.

Heads turned.

Luc took hold of her arm. 'I did not mean to offend . . .'

Sabine bit her lower lip. Then, he saw her tension drain. She resumed her seat.

'I'm sorry,' he said, repeatedly. His hand slipped down her forearm and their fingers interlocked.

She did not reply for a long time. Her big red lips contorted, sadness in her brown eyes sending silver smudges through her black mascara. Luc remained silent while she wiped away at her face.

'The film reminded me of when I was growing up, it brought back some strange feelings.'

For the next hour Luc listened as she poured out her memories.

'My first stone hit Henri square on the forehead, ripping a gash. He said he did not care but I did not believe him. His Triumph bike was the talk of the block. 500 cc's. He smoked dope and was the hardest boy this side of La Vallie. At least that is what he told me. By that time I had spiked my hair and started to wear lipstick. Mama knew she had lost control when I got into studded belts and leather skirts. You should have heard the screaming matches in our house. Mama eventually resigned herself to the fact that I was too far gone to be rededicating my life to Christ. I still had rosary beads trailing over the headboard but that was because I was a Goth. The only prayers I offered up were to Black Sabbath.'

On a hot holiday Monday Sabine and her friends had trailed down a dusty snake of road towards the motor track in Le Mans. They got in on cheap tickets and stood against the flaking whitewash of a concrete stand, their buckles glistening in the sun. Two hours later the race was still droning past. Henri had his fries and Sabine watched the Ricard signs flash. The Rolling Stones were thumping through her headphones, her foot tapping on the back of the seat in front.

All seemed well with the world until the oil-slick of Harkis came rushing through a gap in the fence, steaming through the crowd, flashing iron bars and big white teeth, robbing everyone they could. Sabine saw the race track stewards falling back before the dark surge, falling under the training shoes of their assailants, jaws and skulls cracking amid the flying fists and thrusting metal. Henri stood tall amongst his gang, defending the girls as the hurricane swept over them. The Harkis were grabbing breasts and handbags as they came on, spraying spit and slang, overwhelming Henri and beating him to the ground.

A black hand pulled her hair. Knotted knuckles struck her face and it was there and then that she first felt this deep compulsion to run and keep running until she dropped. Her father was not there to protect her. Henri could not protect her. Who could protect her? Thirty minutes later Sabine stood on the embankment at Les Morlettes thumbing for a lift.

When she did finally return home she found that a clan of asylum seeking Sudanese had infested her block. They would sit around the stairwells and hang over the balconies, skinny bodies stretched out languidly in the heat. Sabine's family were among the few remaining French in the area. Every day they would be harassed for sex by the young and old men alike. Once their mother was beaten for her groceries but the worst came when Sabine had come home from a school trip to find the swirling smoke from a fire pouring out of the flat windows and hear the screams of her mother and sister who were barricaded inside.

When she had finished Sabine's attention was caught by the rain distorted reflection of Notre Dame hunched over the Quai d'Orleans and the piercing glance from the mouldering stone face of Le Stryge looking straight back at her through the darkness.

Sabine took a very deliberate sip of tea and almost threw the cup down in temper. Some Australian tourists got up, paid, and went out the swing door behind them. 'Qu'à cela ne tienne,' she said regretfully and then, 'this is pure self indulgence, please excuse me. It is time for my period!'

'I knew there was something hurting in your heart,' Luc said, 'I could see it in your eyes.'

'I never speak of it,' she murmured.

'I recognised it in you from the first moment I saw you. It's the reason I'm with you. Please never change.'

'Kindred souls?' she said.

'Nothing so passé,' he said. 'Anyway there's no such thing!'

'Then what?'

'You are like one of Wagner's Valkyries!' Luc said. Sabine shook her head.

'You are always so political?'

By around 1pm they were washed up with the brown dregs in the saucers and ushered out onto the street by a tired looking waitress. They stood, desolate in the misty night air. Two slim figures walking over the narrow black bridge. Above them the yellow moon was speared on the sharp cathedral spire as a fine drizzle kept falling like a grey fire curtain over the Île Saint-Louis.

*

Press Cuttings Bureaux:

Brest. Black Metal music concert is infiltrated by narcotics squad.

Saint-Renan. 15th-century church cemetery desecrated by cultist pagans.

Brussels. *Les Joyaux de la Princesse* come-back performance receives rave reviews.

Rennes. A couple seized for selling speeches by Phillipe Henriot and Jean Herold-Paquis.

Nanterre. Three day Student sit-in protests against the college library's banning of books by Alain de Benoist.

Orne. Holiday home set on fire by unidentified regionalist group.

Questembert. The statue of Alain-le-Grand is draped in banners.

Valence. Police report evidence of unspecified 'material' theft from armoury.

Besancon. Three senior officers from the 7th armoured Brigade abscond from the service.

Vichy. Activist's death in police custody leads to martyr's march through the city.

Nancy. TV studio invaded by protestors.

Grenoble. Ring road blockaded by lorry drivers complaining about petrol prices.

Dinant. Printing press confiscated and owner charged for forging identity papers.

Dubai. The Arab League declares the standard price of crude oil at $500 dollars per barrel.

*

A few days later Luc had been contacted by a Russian news channel wanting an interview with a resistance militant. After a number of checks and reassurances a secret meeting was set up. Bardet, Bellew, and Bodine were content that Dubois was the right man for the job. The more traditional wing, who was gaining increasing support as numbers began to flood into the resistance, diluting the hardcore, thought he was not experienced or moderate enough. Bardet's word was final, but there were lingering resentments and if it had not been for an impassioned endorsement from Bellew Luc's participation might not have been approved. In the Au Passage coffee shop where the sound of electro pop all but drowned out his words Luc sat at a corner table with a Rossiya correspondent trying to explain to the reporter why the French people were now turning to sabotage and acts of civil disobedience.

'We need your help too,' he was insisting, as the camera man hovered over him, 'Your nation gave the world Pushkin, Lermontov, Gogol, Dostoevsky, and Tolstoy. You must understand, *La civilization est en peril!*'

His appeal touched a raw nerve with the young staffer. When the piece was aired it made good viewing for the movement, allowing Luc to get his message over without the usual contrived editing designed to paint the resistance in a bad light.

'The young man was sincere and motivated', the correspondent said in his voice-over. 'He only stopped to sip his espresso and on one occasion interrupted his analysis of the current crisis to lend his matches to a pretty chain smoking girl in a leather biker jacket and black sunglasses sitting next to him.'

Indeed, it was noticeable how the lens lingered on Sabine and it forced the Resistance's leadership to reconsider the propaganda asset they had available.

*

'You're blocking us!' Luc screeched. The chairman, Albert Legard, a long-term member whose support had recently swelled following a rash of desertions from the *Union pour un Mouvement Populaire*, bent forward, his tricolor sash folding over his bulbous stomach and struck the table with his gavel.

'Monsieur Dubois, I am calling you to order! I know you are a TV celebrity now but can you kindly confine your remarks to the bookshop accounts, please.'

The other members of the council gathered around in conference began nervously rustling their papers, reports and documents, nodding their assent. The committee of twelve were sitting on a raised platform before an audience of party members. A wave of disquiet rippled through the crowd, raised hands in the hall were overlooked; somewhere from the back of the room someone called for a point of order but was deliberately ignored.

'We've got to change tactics,' Luc repeated, much to the annoyance of the chairman, who wanted him to stick to the agenda. 'Will you not at least consider my paper?' He held up his three-point plan, 'There are copies on the door for all who are interested.'

'Dubois, can you limit your comments to the issue before us?' The chair was spitting teeth. 'Will you take us through the figures for sales and merchandising, please?'

Luc grimaced, picked up his agenda papers, 'Most certainly', he said, then half turning to the auditorium so that it appeared he was addressing them as equals, 'Well, as you can see in-store sales have fallen considerably over the last quarter. This is mainly due to the reduced footfall because of the almost constant harassment visitors get from the Jean Genet types who throw paint and smash our windows on an almost nightly basis . . .' Luc's reference to the author of *Our Lady of the Flowers* caused an outbreak of levity from the assembly. 'This however,' he continued, 'is more than offset by the online trade. A quick look at the figures shows that book, poster, and clothing sales have more than doubled. Bulk orders for leaflets and pamphlets are also doing very well and more than compensating for shortfalls elsewhere.'

'I notice there has been a threefold increase in staff expenses', Legard said, trying to combat the triumphalist tone of Luc's delivery.

'Unfortunately one of the consequences of the shop's high visibility is that our staff sometimes need to use taxis or private hire cars to ensure their safety. I think it is a good investment.'

'That is for this committee to decide', Legard cut in. This drew hisses from the now sympathetic audience who were most concerned that activists did not shoulder risks above and beyond what was absolutely necessary.

Luc threw up his hands. 'I think you have your answer?'

'And you can stop playing to the gallery,' Legard barked, 'this is not England, here we debate and use reason to formulate strategy not play the populist card to win over the masses.'

'And maybe that is why we are still a fringe organisation with a pool of latent support?'

This threw Legard off balance. Some of the local council members were becoming agitated with the way the meeting was going. Legard sensed he was losing them and lashed out condescendingly. 'Learn your history, young man, do you not remember Agincourt and Crecy?'

'Yes, the English won because we employed the wrong tactics. Get over it. The problem facing all of us now is a new dark age sweeping down over Europe. Are we to fight our neighbours again and again? Are we going to repeat the Sun King's stupidity and send cannons to break down the walls of Vienna?' Luc paused for a second to build the effect, 'Or are we going to swallow our parochial pride and ride to glory alongside Sobieski's winged hussars?'

This brought the crowd to its feet. Clapping hands rolled like thunder through the dark.

1968 Revisited

he lecture theatre's benches were like a wall of faces, students overflowing onto the steps and flooding the aisles, sitting on window-sills and blocking doorways. The young orator stood on the platform, hands in pockets, blonde hair shining in the spotlight. Then his thin lips opened.

'My friends,' he said, leaning into the microphone, 'all around us the old order is decaying, their corruption is everywhere, on our TVs, in the factories, and walking our streets!' A wave of clapping. 'This is our time. For half a century these liars, hypocrites, criminals, and traitors have turned our land into a desolation. They feed like parasites on a rotting corpse...' More clapping. 'They have made strangers of us in our own land.' A tumultuous response. 'Their oppressive laws prevent us from saying anything, doing anything or seeing anything they do not want us to... they tie us up in the immoral correctness of their ways... make our normal instincts seem abnormal and vile . . . even turn us against our own families and friends . . . How did it come to this? Our press is not free; our universities do not educate, they indoctrinate; and our media pours out platitudes about inane celebrities and game shows while people are dragged off to prison for giving voice to the truth . . . Where is the France of Montaigne? Where is the land of Racine?

'Comrades, we have outgrown the old terminologies. A new millennium demands a new credo!' The speaker rubbed his hands. 'We have support in the cities, in the countryside, amongst the bourgeois and the workers . . . we even have cadres here in the university!' The young and confident were by now shouting support, raising their voices for the first time, exalting in the liberation of their own feelings.

Luc bent towards Sabine as they sat together in the front row facing two men and a girl in military-style leather jackets. 'Now that's the kind of energy that gets people off their arses,' he said, 'What have our enemies got to match this?'

'Nothing,' said Sabine, 'they have lost the intellectual argument and soon they will lose the streets.'

Luc leaned in even closer, whispering intently, 'You know', he said, unlocking his hands and raising one circling finger to point out the auditorium about them. 'Even as recently as five years ago these people would have been filled with the spirit of 68.'

'Looks like we've found the vaccination for that madness', Sabine smiled.

When Laurent Bardet finished he invited people from the audience to stand up, shout out their name and what they were studying before asking a question. With each reply the applause from the platform steps to the upper balcony resounded louder and more earnestly. After fifteen minutes the speaker reached for a glass of water.

'Guys', Laurent said, 'This is a life and death struggle your children need you to win.'

The audience rose in a mass, their noisy support echoing in a rotating rhythm around the drum like theatre. Afterwards people filed out into the night, all fired up.

*

In the institute corridor, the next day, a student wearing a hammer and sickle badge stopped Luc in his tracks.

'Comrade Dubois, can we have a word?'

'Certainly *tovarich*', Luc laughed, 'lead the way.' His hand gestured easy-going acceptance.

In a social sciences seminar room on the top floor, at a long mahogany table under a portrait of Adorno, sat Gilles Renard, a Betar leader on campus. He was smoking slowly, holding a cigarette firmly to his lips and looking at Luc through the smoke.

'Listen Dubois, I have a headache', he said, rather dismissively. His chin was resting in his hand, elbow propped on the rosewood. Luc could see his face reflected in the window over Renard's shoulder, a single electric bulb casting his image in incongruous shadows against the sunset. Renard shook the ash from his cigarette, his fingers drumming on the polished surface. 'Your faction', he hesitated to give it a name, 'are beginning to concern us. Members of the faculty are giving me certain instructions. I'm sure you understand.'

Luc's face showed no surprise or emotion. He walked casually over to the table, shook a Gitane out of a half empty packet from the inside pocket of his jacket, bent towards Renard and taking his forearm in a tight grip, lit his own cigarette from the dying embers of the one being held by his would be interrogator. The tip turned red as Luc sucked. Then exhaling deeply, 'We don't care about your instructions,' he said, 'your people are an anachronism. We won't live in your gulags anymore . . . !'

*

In that moment open warfare was declared. It began with sporadic fistfights in the quadrangles but soon spilt over into pitched battles wherever people gathered. Lectures by Trotskyists were broken up when traditionalist students stormed meeting rooms, throwing chairs and slashing with bicycle chains. Other professors cancelled classes on the slightest pretext and, after three days of constant disruption, the Dean harangued the feuding groups from the chapel steps. It became obvious to the anxious university authorities that the scenario was beginning to polarise popular opinion. There was a real danger of the college becoming the touch paper for mass civil disorder. The opposing sides facing off in the Boulevard Saint-Michel led to police reinforcements being called in to seal off the approach roads in an effort to contain any fighting. It was rumoured that Ministers were beginning to worry. Commissaire Barrineau, head of the Paris constabulary, had been called in to Ben Hassi's office. The Head of Interior Justice was in a fearful state as he flicked through the Commissaire's report.

'Crush these agitators Barrineau', he said, 'otherwise I will move my *Mujahidin* into the city!'

Later that week, under direct orders of the Committee for Equality, a column of helmeted police, armed with shields and truncheons, marched under the college arch and attacked anyone waving a tri-color, bundling boys and girls into the back of black, shuttered trucks. Some desperate types fought back and got close enough to see their friends through the wire mesh windows of the CRS vans. Onlookers jeered and office workers waved angry fists. Some-one threw a metal railing and a windscreen shat-tered. The next moment a police transport swerved into a building, the driver fell out the door, blood streaming from his face. Rushing to free their col-leagues, students beat on the sides of vehicles, chanting 'State Oppression!' Then a gas grenade went off, followed by another and a water cannon lashed out sending young bodies flying backwards through clouds of smoke.

*

They were already scuffling on the staircase. Sabine could hear hysterical shouting reaching fever pitch. She began shredding papers and deleting sensitive files as the door to the office flew off its hinges and the CRS streamed in, forcing party workers up against the wall, frisking the building's occupants for concealed weaponry.

'Bastards!' she heard someone curse, then felt the barrel of an automatic rifle poke her in the back and turned just in time to see a biracial with big ivory teeth close in on her face.

A butt hit Luc in the gut, dropping him panting to the floor as the security forces pulled out their computers, swept up paper files into big black bin liners, and scoured drawers for letters, disks, and back-up tapes.

'I want it all!' said their commander. He was wearing a helmet with a built in microphone and a transparent visor; a blue flak jacket labelled with his

surname, Calman; a webbed belt and padded leg-
gings. Sabine noticed the flicker of enmity in his
green eyes. This went beyond duty; it was personal.
He stood a head taller than the others and was
clearly enjoying the task. 'Now who's in charge
here?' When it became obvious no one was going to
respond he pulled Sabine away from the molesta-
tions of his trooper and forced her down onto her
knees in front of him. 'I will ask you once more.
Who is in charge?' Again silence. Calman's gloved
hand unclipped his holster and pulled a Pamas G1
from its leather casement. 'I will count to three', he
said, pointing the weapon to his victim's temple,
'Remember, in times like these it is easy to justify a
death. Prisoners are frequently shot for resisting
arrest.'

'I am in charge', Luc said breathlessly from the
ground.

'Name?'

'Luc Dubois . . .'

'Take him', said the officer, clipping the automatic pistol back into place and ramming Sabine's
head against the side of a desk, 'Bitch!' They
scooped Luc up off the carpet and bundled him
down the staircase. 'I want all their ID's', he ordered, then turning to the people up against the
wall, 'Play with fire and you will get burned!'

Afterwards, picking up counter revolutionary
treatises by Joseph de Maistre and Louis de Bonald,
replacing the torn posters the security services had
flung to the ground, Sabine went over to the window
just in time to see Luc taking a rabbit punch to the
kidney as he was bent double into a car and driven
off towards the Prefecture de Police. In the road a
column of CRS were loading seized materials into
the back of a truck. A group of spectators had gathered and some press men were taking photos.

*

Upon release, it took Luc six, maybe seven hours to find his way home. Dominique Pascale, a small red-haired activist, formerly of Inspecteur Fouvier's own branch of the secret service, had come to sit with Sabine. Around midnight the doorbell rang and he staggered across the threshold, pale and shivering. Dominique folded her copy of *Nouvelle Revue* and left. Sabine sat him down on the edge of the bed. At first he rambled circuitously, then angry memories poured out.

'They are desperate to destroy our influence amongst the students'. Sabine wiped the drool from his mouth. 'The cops gave me a beating in the car and another at the station.' Sabine took a hand and stroked it gently. 'A little man with bushy eyebrows questioned me for a while. I can't remember his name but it sounded foreign. He was toying with an old-fashioned pocket watch on a gold link chain. Then when he got bored he said he'd heard enough and warned me off getting involved with street politics. That's when they came back and punched me around the room again. I lost consciousness and woke up when one of them stood over me and undid his zip.'

'Non!' Sabine objected.

'There you are', the policeman said, 'what will the girls say when they smell that?'

She helped him over to the bathroom and he turned on the shower, slipping out of his stained clothes and letting the warm water cascade over his shoulders. Sabine leaned back on the basin and watched him through the shining glass capsule, the jetting water enveloping him in its spray.

Luc opened his mouth, the nozzle rinsing his gums, dislodging blood clots. Blue bruising mottled his ribs like a marbled steak, already turning yellow around his sternum where the skin was grazed and split by knuckle-knotted gouges. He rubbed himself dry with a soft towel Sabine had handed him through the sliding door; his aching body felt fresh and clean. Then she held out a razor. He studied his jaw in the misty mirror and caught the familiar stare of those lone lupine eyes. 'The strength of the pack is the wolf,' he recited to himself, 'and the strength of the wolf is the pack.'

'And soon we will hunt!' his companion said.

*

Despite the seizures they decided to keep the mood of violence alive in the Latin Quarter. First by attacking the Sorbonne office of One World Action, tearing out the communications network and torching the room, then spraying the Place de la Sorbonne, the little square overhung by the university's dome, with their spider-like symbols. Franck Bodine was organising actions all over the city. Arnaud Bellew issued press releases from a new secret operations centre on the Rue Etienne Dolet in Belleville:

> The current spate of politically motivated arrests and the illegal crackdown on our legitimate democratic activities will not disrupt our campaign. We anticipated State totalitarianism and have taken appropriate measures to ensure the continuity of our movement . . .

This message was relayed by all media and signed Charlemagne 21. Within hours, Said Ben Hassi appeared on the TV news channels alongside The Puppet President, Monsieur Belaire, to denounce this new development, promising to root out the evil. Belaire just nodded ascent, eager to retain the block vote Ben Hassi had promised in the coming elections.

As part of the Resistance's counter offensive, Sabine got up early the next morning, leaving Luc in bed and made her way to a pre-arranged *rendez-vous*. There were three others standing in front of the café, hands thrust deep into their pockets, shivering in the grey morning air. Sabine knew only one of them, André Morel, a bank clerk from Chambord. He was wearing a black bomber jacket and a woollen hat pulled down tight over his flaxen hair. He introduced her to Patrice, a thick-set veteran of the movement, his white, round face sporting a ragged, red suture scar. Sabine noticed a black rat tattoo on his forearm as they shook hands. Then there was Anton. He was very young, all angular and bravado thin like rice paper. At one point he produced a blade from his pocket and was told firmly to put it away unless prepared to use it. He complied with the order, his wet eyes cloudy with humiliation.

André had the leaflets in a blue sports bag. Sabine helped André share out the bundles, each of them stuffing the glossy papers into plastic carriers or inside their coats. Soon they had spread out across Boulevard Raspail, each taking his allotted route along the streets. Sabine progressed rapidly, some of the houses and shops had letter boxes which made her task easier, in other cases she left five or six leaflets scattered conspicuously on stairwells or tenement notice boards.

Slowly but surely the occupants began to stir. She could hear mothers calling to sulky children, the sound of crockery clattering at breakfast tables. Avoiding the mounds of dog excrement on the broken pavements, Sabine was eventually confronted by a fat old man standing on his doorstep.

'Bitch!' he called after her, 'You should be ashamed of yourself!' She carried on, determined to avoid distraction. 'Our fathers and grandfathers fought a war against pigs like you!'

On the Rue Boissonade, she walked straight into a police patrol. Stepping into a doorway at the last moment and pretending to ring the bell as they walked past, Sabine waited watchfully until they disappeared from view.

At the far end of Edgar Quinet, the group gathered as agreed around Brancusi's statue of *The Kiss*. André had previously produced a computer graphic of the Hotel Aiglon, which the Islamists had recently commandeered.

'It would be a real coup if we could get inside,' he smiled mischievously, 'They will never expect that!' The group moved across cemetery Montparnasse, Patrice and Anton fanning out to the east and west corners to act as look-outs while André and Sabine made towards the steps leading up from the pavement to the big ornate doorway. Both Patrice and Anton signalled the all clear. They mounted towards the marble portico. An armed guard twisted to face them as Sabine heard a shout and saw Patrice running, followed by a red-faced policeman coming around the corner of the building shaking one of their leaflets in the air. André realised the game was up and swung his bag into the groin of the robed sentry who had stepped forward to challenge them. Then both he and Sabine scattered in opposite directions.

André looked back, just in time to see one of the cops catch up to Patrice and tackle him around the legs. They were still rolling around on the ground as others came up to grab his compatriot's extremities, pinning him to the floor. For a second André almost stopped, considering the option to go back to help, but he heard Sabine's high-pitched scream:

'Run . . . ! Run . . . !'

André saw the police bounce Patrice's head a few times on the stonework before kicking him in the chest. He turned, speeding into a galleria and disappeared into a maze of small shops. Sabine was panting heavily, swivelling around sharp concrete corners, staying maybe twenty-five metres ahead of her pursuers.

'C'mon', she gasped, regretting all those cigarettes, 'you can do it!' The next thing she realised was that a man was lunging for her and she was slipping onto her knees, tearing her jeans, lifting herself on bleeding hands, kicking his grasping fingers away, shouting at the passers-by that she was 'Political, not criminal!' and watched them step aside not wanting to get involved.

She broke her way through a chain of commuters crossing Rue Foidevaux and took a look over her shoulder. There was only one policeman in view and he was talking into a radio as he chased her across Square George Lamarque. On the Place Denfert Rochereau Sabine drew up at a bus stop and stepped aboard just as it pulled away down René Coty. Her lungs were bursting. Collecting herself, she stared out of the back window, the policeman was lost in a sea of citizens, gesticulating wildly, asking if anyone had seen a girl running this way, his angry face shrinking into the crowd.

At the next stop she got off, dumped her coat in a waste bin and took a taxi back to Belleville. She entered the building fully expecting to find André already there.

'Were you followed?' demanded Bellew, his face creased by anxiety. A glance to his personal bodyguard ensured a patrol was sent out to reconnoitre the streets outside.

'No, I made sure . . . '

'What about André?'

'Got away.'

'Patrice and Anton?'

'They got Patrice in Cemetery Montparnasse but he'll never talk, he's not the type.' Sabine stayed for a long time, stalking the corridors, waiting for André to call. The rooms were full of water bottles, papers, and munitions. Franck Bodine was creating an arsenal for the next phase of the insurrection. He was very busy but made a point of coming to see if she was all right.

'You and Luc are two of our best militants', he said as he bathed her grazed palms and she drank some peppermint tea. One hour later André phoned to say he was safe. Relieved, Sabine left for home, skipping down the spiral stairwell. As she did she looked up through a half open door to see a serious middle-aged man with a red dragon *motif* stitched into an olive green army shirt hunched over a computer screen. There was a cigarette hanging from his lip as he tapped away furiously at the keyboard. Bodine who was accompanying her down the stairs saw the look of curiosity on her face.

'Meibion Glyndwr,' he said, 'Pays de Galles'.

Holy Virgin

A young woman dressed as Joan of Arc sat astride a white horse before the crowd. She waved a silver sword that sliced down through the clear blue air, drawing a roar of approval from the marchers in front of the Hotel de Ville. Behind her, the column gathered momentum like some great anaconda, snaking between the tall buildings, advancing down the middle of the road under a canopy of tricolors. Besides the proud veterans in berets were women with babes in arms and interspersed between them the young bloods in black jackets emblazoned with Celtic crosses—toughs in sunglasses walking side by side with their Belgian, Flemish and Italian comrades. The raucous chanting mounted to a crescendo:

Marchons, Marchons!
Qu'un sang impur
Abreuve nos sillons!

Young girls in red, white, and blue sashes ran along the pavement handing out freshly printed leaflets. Up on the rooftops TV cameras were filming and state security servicemen hung precariously over balconies trying to identify known agitators so that the snatch-squads could move in. The Rue de Rivoli was at a standstill, car horns sounding in support, deafening klaxons echoing off the press of flesh and concrete.

A crowd of several thousand counter-demonstrators had congregated under the Ché Guevara and *SoS Racisme* flags of Gilles Renard, many from the *banlieues* at Villiers-le-Bel. They had also gathered on the Tuileries to oppose the march. As the nationalists passed, someone fired a pistol into the air. For a moment there was pandemonium and a riot was only narrowly avoided when the police formed up into a solid phalanx to keep the rival crowds apart. At Place de Concord, more of Renards' leftist provocateurs threw stones and this time the CRS made a baton charge which scattered the rioters into the nearby side streets. On the Voie Georges Pompidou mounted units charged back and forth for almost an hour forcing the two sides off the open ground. The buzzing blue sirens of ambulances and red flash of Europol militia personnel carriers filled the air.

At the Esplanade des Invalides Laurent Bardet mounted the podium in the centre of the square. The wooden frame was festooned with flowers. The marchers came past, dipping their regional flags, a man in a blue suit stood at a nearby lectern calling out the names of the provinces as they processed, 'Allez Lorraine, La Champagne approche!'

Standing in front of the microphone, surrounded by his people, Bardet, in a smart black suit, white shirt, and wine red tie, surveyed the scene before him. Below, covering the steps were his Praetorian guard, fanatically loyal. To his right were a large group of pregnant women and to his left others with empty baby carriages. There was no subtlety, only the desire to get the point across. France was in demographic meltdown.

'Welcome my dear compatriots,' he said loudly, 'Welcome to the celebration the Eurabists and Barbouzards wanted to ban and forget about!' He waved his hand at the multitudes around the podium. 'And you see they have failed . . . and why have they failed? Because we refuse to forget . . . we will never forget who we are, why we are, or where we are going!' Wave upon wave of applause greeted his every utterance. 'But why, why stop it? Because it is a symbolic day of national celebration! A day when we the defenders of the sacred flame that burns in the heart of France gather en masse to warm ourselves beside the fire of patriotic memories. You see, it is we who uphold the inaliable rights of man, liberty, property, security, and resistance to oppression . . . and it is we who will continue to defend these ideals to the very last breath in our bodies.' He gripped the podium with both hands, 'today it is we who stand in the eye of the storm. It is we who fight against the tyranny of imported disorder and violence, we who oppose the commodification of our culture, the reign of usury, and the demands of minorities who impose their values over us.' Laurent waved his arms, 'Neither Monsieur le President, nor his Minister for Interior Justice or their baying hordes from Africa stand for France. They may mouth our national anthem, but I for one am not fooled, are you?'

'Non!' came back the answer.

'Our language is spoken on five continents, our entrepreneurship and scientific expertise leads the fields of nuclear technology and the aerospace industry. Ours is a nation synonymous worldwide with culture. We are a land of ideas, debate, thinkers, and philosophers not dictatorial feudal imams . . . And that is why it is WE who must build barricades against this coming age of darkness. It is we who hold the torch of hope aloft in the world . . . And why it is we, this very generation, who will decide if France lives or perishes. There can be no retreat, no surrender, because capitulation to this new wave of zealotry and barbarism will lead to annihilation. Look to tomorrow through the lessons of our past. The martyrdom of thousands upon thousands of Christian Europeans from Otranto to Kosovo field. It is a struggle for our very existence and we will survive!'

This last statement was met by spontaneous outbursts of enthusiastic support. Bardet was walking about the platform acknowledging shouts from the crowd when a single deadly shot rang out and his body toppled over the balustrade onto the ground. At first there was shock and then panic as people fled in all directions leaving a cohort of clean cut muscular young men in sports jackets to form a square around their fallen leader.

La semaine sanglante

By evening the city was in flames and fires were advancing street by broken street, driving the stain-faced French out of their homes, thousands fleeing like refugees from a war zone. Families scurried away with whatever essentials they could carry, toiletries, battered suitcases, plastic bags full of frozen food and bottled water. Behind them the sky glowed red over blackened rooftops and mobs wielding glinting machetes sliced through the smoke and sparking embers.

Gilles Renard's student Marxists so buoyed up on egalitarian rhetoric and Trotskyite theory earlier in the day now looked on with shock and awe at the storm being unleashed. Like everyone else, they were anxious about being overtaken on the road and beaten to death. Panic spread like contagion. Small groups of frightened cowering people were ducking and weaving between burnt out cars, babies crying, grandmothers struggling beside wide-eyed teenagers. Occasionally, a punctured petrol tank would ignite, sending burning geysers of fuel up into the warm orange air. And in the distance the drums echoing through the alleys and coming down off the rooftops, that incessant rhythmic beat, the samba soundtrack to the mayhem.

Sabine was down amongst the frightened population in the streets watching as the police came running, shooting, then falling back. The insurgents advanced inexorably towards la Cité. People jostled in their desperation to escape them, penned in ever closer to the river. She looked back and saw that the mob coming down from La Fayette had set fire to the church of Notre-Dame de L'Assomption. The congregation, who had sought sanctuary inside now ran into the square where they were beaten and robbed. A police cordon on the corner of Place Vendôme was being pushed further and further back towards the Ministry of Justice, where Ben Hassi sat rubbing his hands and his ever-faithful Private Secretary Alphonse Belan quivered in anticipation of the celebratory acts of buggery that would ensue. Shiny black personnel carriers were being rocked back and forth by a sea of rioters pouring out of Place de la Madeleine. On Rue Royale, mounted officers careered up against a mud slide of black attackers, wave after wave rippling endlessly towards the Fontaine des Fleuves. They kept coming like mindless lemmings leaping across an apocalyptic shore of burning asphalt. The battle backlit by the red flares of erupting Molotov cocktails - reflecting off helmets and visors while matchstick-thin arsonists in balaclavas stood silhouetted against the skyline.

'The indignation of the people is glorious to be-
hold!' Ben Hassi laughed, smug about his premedi-
tated uprising.

*

Sabine had ended up in an unfamiliar district.
Around her, the sound of fighting and the blistered
faces of abandoned houses screamed the arrival of
civil war. She followed others rushing mindlessly
across a narrow courtyard. Some CRS men, taking
shelter from the storm breaking out all around
them, stood drinking beer from a looted supermarket. They paid no attention as the civilians dashed
away, casting long shadows against the metal
screens pulled down to protect shop windows. Out
of the corner of her eye, Sabine saw the glistening
brown face of a man in flowing white robes squatting in a doorway with an automatic weapon laid
across his knees. Above, a black flag waved boldly
and triumphantly against a sliver of moon.

After Bardet's assassination, Luc had lost touch
with Sabine in the melée, but had made it back
safely to their apartment. He knew Bodine and
Bellew had contingency plans and had arranged to
rendez-vous with them later. Now his thoughts were
on Sabine. Night had fallen since his return and she
had not come home. The Paris streetlights were
flickering along the quai. Over in the Quartier, Luc
could hear percussion grenades and the crack of
small arms fire back and forth along the Left Bank.
From their balcony he could smell the tear gas floating across the Pont de la Tournelle and watched as
two squad cars of police were overwhelmed by
brigands waving sticks, surging towards the Île's
Quai de Bethune.

Catching his breath, Luc unbuttoned his jacket,
slipped a short-barrelled .38 out of a shoulder hol-

ster and checked its action by levering the hammer with his thumb. He then shot a nervous Robert de Niro smile at the bedroom mirror and, mimicking the scene from *Taxi Driver*, asked 'Are you looking at me?' before rushing down the stairway to the street.

He strode across the cobbled square directly outside the entrance and was almost immediately surrounded by a scene more reminiscent of Conrad's *Heart of Darkness* than Zola's *L'Assommoir*. A chanting circle of demonic charcoal covered bodies, all whirling torsos and stabbing blades, materialised out of the smoke, forming an undulating barrier between him and the river. Luc swivelled to see if the snake had a head. One, grinning indolently, pushed an insulting face to within striking distance, its tongue rolling over thick lips. Luc pointed his weapon right between the eyes mocking him. For a moment he thought he would have to fire, but just as his finger tightened on the metal, the band scattered, and he breathed a sigh of relief. Walking through the city, he spotted vandals throwing kerosene flares through apartment windows and others loading anything they could into carjacked vehicles.

Just before midnight, Luc was sidling around a dark courtyard in Saint Sulpice, and looking at the bloodied faces gathered there, searching for Sabine.

'Fifty Euro,' a voice behind him offered.

Luc turned. Lecherous black eyes stared back above a beard

'Fifty Euro?'

At first Luc thought he was being mugged by a drug addict, but soon realised his tormentor was unarmed.

'Forty, then?' the man continued, throwing open a door, 'Cheap at the price!'

Luc looked inside to see a line of eight or nine year old girls tied naked to the wall. On a makeshift bed a man forcing himself between two pale female legs.

'They're all nice and young!' the bearded man said, 'Fresh French girls!'

Luc shook his head in disgust.

'I'll make sure she has douche before you fuck her.'

Luc moved away.

'Thirty Euro. My last offer, they won't struggle, not after I . . . ' His hands made a sweeping movement, imitating a slap, and Luc retreated into the darkness, only just overcoming the temptation to kill the pimp where he stood.

For several hours Sabine wandered through the back streets, occasionally skirting roistering gangs, strutting drunkenly along the centre of the road. From a distance she saw a man walking in circles around a naked body on the Place de Clichy. He held a torn dress in one hand and a curved dagger in the other. The look of joy on his face was unmistakable. A few small fires had been started in Rue de Leningrad and groups of people warmed themselves over the flaring red tinder. Avoiding these, Sabine made her way across the nexus of streets to the south, trying to find refuge in one of the deserted buildings.

As she picked her way along Des Batignolles, Sabine noticed even the dilapidated buildings had been barricaded before being deserted, sometimes with a tangle of twisted wires, other times with bolted grilles. Everything was covered with a fine coating of ash. Even the metal-domed church, which wore a mask of glowing embers, was caught for a moment in the glimmer of signal rockets and sweeping helicopter beams. After the initial violence, she could see the looting was taking on a more organised form. Outside the Musée Cerusschi, a white van was being filled with stolen *objets d'art*. Bongo drummers whipped dancers into a trance on the steps outside Lycée Chaptal.

Halfway down Rue De Courcelles, Sabine looked over her shoulder as a group of men appeared on the corner of Place Chassaigne. They shouted and pointed at her as she moved in the shadows from door to door. She broke into a full sprint but another troop approached from the front. A white-suited man was in command, standing at the gang's nucleus, his arms waving them on. Sabine span on her heels and changed trajectory, making diagonally across Faubourg St. Honore. A star-shell zoomed up into the sky from the deck of a police boat and illuminated the whole street in a cascading effervescence. Sabine stopped, out of breath, backing helplessly into a shop entrance as the gangs closed in on her. Then, through feline eyes, she saw the man in the white suit unbuckling his trousers.

*

In the Quartier men and women of all ages crowded the stairwells, eager to join the resistance. Hundreds of youths, tricolor patches sewn hastily on their jackets had stormed an arsenal at the local police commissariat and helped themselves to automatic weapons and boxes of ammunition. In the crooked streets around Lycée Louis Le grand these volunteers seemed to be everywhere, black-jacketed young men surging into the streets, disarming the lacklustre police patrols and forcing a small Europol Militia convoy to halt in Rue Saint-Jacques.

They threw up makeshift street barricades. Large numbers of people came out to form columns, passing anything and everything along a human chain to build a defensive line. Men in shirts, sleeves rolled up to their elbows stood toe-to-toe with young women in pencil-slim skirts and Louis Vuitton shoes, each trying to out-do the other in the effort to survive.

Reports on the radio that a black Mercedes daubed with a red tyr rune was driving around Place de La Bastille, guns bristling out of windows, raised hopes of a fightback. Bodine and Bellew were on the barricades, hard expressions framed against fluttering flags with Celtic crosses. Behind them, fanatical men in green combat jackets stood in the glow of burning buildings, cocking machine pistols.

'Well Franck, looks like you got your war!' Bellew said, pointing at the red skyline.

'This is not the time or the place of my choosing!'

'We can hold these streets and save lives until some form of normality returns.'

'I think the riots are a cover,' Bodine said. 'This is too well organised. We are facing a *coup d'état*, not sporadic violence.'

When the rioting hordes came from the Marais they were met by constant fire from a café on the Square Albert Schweitzer. Police footage later showed the former undercover agent and now resistance fighter Dominique Pascale with a Fara 83 assault rifle shooting out of an upstairs window. And when CRS engineers tried to seal off the Place des Vosges with razor wire indignant residents came out to confront them.

*

A dark stain of blue smoke hung over the Île de la Cité. Towering buildings had been gutted, majestic statues toppled, government offices ransacked. Luc thought of how the barbarians had stormed Rome. Hooded mobs were running through the streets. They gathered in the squares and market places, chanting 'Ben Hassi for President! Ben Hassi for President!' With the hordes pouring down the boulevards citizens locked themselves in their homes. Some made makeshift weapons from kitchen utensils and garden tools. The crowds cheerfully smashed windows and planted their green-and-red banners on rooftops. In the Champs De Mars, one zealot held a woman by the hair and beat her mouth with his fist. Her blonde boyfriend lay dead by her side as the assailant swung his fiancée's head down hard on the pavement, cracking her skull, smashing her white teeth

The rioters began setting fire to any home that barred their doors or refused to give up their women. The smell of roasting human flesh billowed out from the windows. Swarming through Les Halles, they made towards the Quai Du Louvre, where a Republican Prefect had fortified his residence and armed his small retinue of secret service officers. The dark-eyed rioters saw a white flag of surrender emerge from a balcony above the Residency. The civil servants, under strict orders, did not fire their weapons. Maurice Deville, the Republican delegate for the First Arrondissement came out onto the steps to face the storm of anger sweeping through the city, his adversaries brandishing torches and curved weaponry of all descriptions. Deville's face looked confused in the dusk. The crowd howled and jeered at the sight of him.

'We are all Frenchmen!' he called, 'Stop this bloodshed!'

With that the mass swarmed like locusts upon a cornfield and the senator was lost in a flurry of striking steel.

That same moment, a black Renault Vel Satis swung out of the Interior Ministry and pushed its way through the crowds milling around Place Beauvau. The *mujahidin*, alerted by a call from colleagues, strode out in their loose-fitting robes, firing their guns in the air to clear a path through the surrounding streets.

A hundred metres along the road, the Renault swerved under a massive stone portico leading to the Elysées Palace. Here too the *mujahidin* fighters were prominently placed, standing alongside the two white-gloved *Gardes Republicains* in the sentry boxes. There the car temporarily halted, the guard bending to salute the occupants before waving them through. Drawing up on the forecourt beyond the metal gates, two of the President's senior officials stood patiently on the gravel, waiting while Said Ben Hassi took a long-distance call from General Malek, a Wahabi fundamentalist who had recently seized power in Riyadh. Then, opening the doors for the minister and his private secretary, they respectfully chaperoned them through a side door into the Palace. Before penetrating any further into the corridors of power, however, they were made to wait a few moments in the vestibule, lingering under a crystal chandelier, awaiting clearance to proceed. Ben Hassi shook his head and Belan smiled.

'Delays like this will soon be behind us, Minister!'

Belan saw a flash of teeth from his master. 'I'll have the Kuffar's head for such an insult!'

They moved on up the granite stairs to the first floor and then down a wide landing before gaining entrance into the Salon des Ordonnances. An orange glow shone through the large windows, trails of smoke from the fires on the Champs Elysées, only three hundred metres away, drifted by in the air. The President's own personal secretary Peter Stein greeted Ben Hassi and his slim companion and peer, Alphonse Belan, with a genuine broad smile.

'Monsieur le Ministre . . . '

'Peter' Ben Hassi gestured warmly, 'I am expected, I believe?'

'*Oui*, President Belaire is looking forward to your audience.'

There was a muffled assent from beyond the door and Ben Hassi stepped inside the President's private study leaving Stein and Belan to flirt in the antechamber.

'Masaa El-Khair, Said,' President Belaire chirped charmingly, getting out of his seat and giving the traditional finger to mouth bowing gesture of welcome to which Ben Hassi was accustomed. 'Of course, you already know Adva Cohen, the hedge fund manager,' gesturing to the old magnate seated in a leather chair before a fire.

'*Bon soir*,' the sitting man said, reaching forward to put a cup down on a small table.

'Please make yourself comfortable.' The President was in an affable mood.

Ben Hassi circled Belaire, his shoes treading warily on the Savonnerie carpet, suspiciously casting an eye out of the window, observing his men brandishing their Kalashnikovs under the lime and beech trees below. Eventually, after managing to make the President feel thoroughly uncomfortable in his own private rooms, he took a chair in front of glass-fronted bookshelves filled with first editions of classic French texts.

'Coffee?' the President asked.

'Champagne, I think,' replied the Moroccan 'After all, gentlemen, should we not be celebrating?'

'Indeed,' Cohen cackled through glittering pearl dentures. 'I trust you have both had electronic confirmation of the transfer of the funds we agreed?'

Both men nodded assent.

'Good,' Cohen continued, 'And now gentlemen, may I take this opportunity to quote Victor Hugo?' A cynical smile cracked his salty lips. 'There is nothing like a dream to create the future.' The irony was not lost on his co-conspirators and they raised glasses in a show of false unity.

'Indeed, we have fulfilled Jean Raspail's prophecy,' Ben Hassi confirmed. 'Like our Policy Institute front organisations and our NGO's, they will contrive to use Western taxes to support your starving and poor, isn't that right Belaire?'

'Assurement, not just in France but across all of Western Europe, until the population transition is complete.'

A second bottle was opened, the cork popping in the silence.

'Look outside,' Cohen said, 'tonight we have created Haiti in the centre of Paris, our power is growing stronger and stronger.'

They clinked glasses and stood looking out over the burning city.

'Magnificent, isn't it,' he said.

'I foresee a new Constantinople rising from the ashes, a western Byzantium,' Belaire said, nodding. Ben Hassi looked askance.

'A European Mecca,' he corrected the President, 'I have sworn it for my grandchildren!'

*

By the following morning, the fires had still not been quelled and the police had been driven off again. The mob had taken over whole sections of the city. Luc had spent a largely sleepless night staring out over the rooftops, cut off from Bodine's forces, thinking how to motivate his action unit and fight back before any more atrocities could be committed. He came down a narrow curling staircase from a casement overlooking the Rue Thouin and emerged into a chamber where a small group of blood-stained men and women were clinging together, more in hope than self-belief.

'How many?' he said.

'Only twenty three,' said a brooding young man, olive jacket hanging loosely from wire-thin shoulders, 'but we're fully armed and fed.'

Luc could see the residue of a cooked breakfast spread out on a table.

'Come on,' he said, lifting a knife to his eye, checking the sharpness of the serrated edge, 'We need to get out of here.'

The Unit filed out of the doorway, backs against the wall, eyes on the street corners and adjacent rooftops. They fanned out down Rue Descartes making for Place Maubert. When they came up to the Pontau Double, the bridge was empty, just rubbish blowing around and a body or two sprawled out on the road. Slowly they covered the ground between Quai de Gesvres and Quai de la Megisserie, frayed nerves and curling fingers circling triggers. In Place du Louvre they came across the severed head of Maurice Deville planted firmly on a stake in front of his residence. An expression of utter shock remained fixed on the senator's patrician face, his blank eyes staring out on a Paris he no longer knew or recognised. Some of Luc's troop vomited when they saw the flies buzzing out from the bloody hole between the lolling tongue and swollen lips, their nostrils catching the sweet smell of the politician's putrescence.

'A fool's reward for one of this city's biggest fools!' Luc spat.

Just then a small group of immigrants came around the corner of the Palais du Louvre and, before he could stop them, his men, fired up by the sight of murder and mayhem, charged across St. Germain L'Auxeroiss. When the rabble saw the ravenous werewolves howling for revenge, they broke and ran, dropping their weapons.

*

For the first seventy-two hours the indigenous population openly aided the resistance, hurling bottles and broken furniture at the rioters and the CRS Mobile. From radio and TV sources it became clear that the army was moving in to surround the city. Bodine's people were fighting to break out of the potential noose the Minister of Interior Justice was planning for them.

Military scout cars with Eurabic pennants appeared through the rolling smoke in Rond Point des Champs-Elysées, levelling steady fire on buildings suspected of harbouring resisters. At the same time, a column of tanks rumbled up Avenue Matignon, their turrets shooting at anything that moved. Gendamerie helicopters hovered low over Quai D'Orsay as Bodine's sharpshooters returned fire from rooftops, trying to hold off the government forces. No one expected the rioters to be punished. The whole tone of the state propaganda machine focused on the violence of the resistance and their supporters and spun the story to imply the rioters had only reacted to racist provocation. Over the next few hours there were brief lulls in the battle, but scattered sniping fire resumed from the rooftops encircling the Odeon. When Luc and his people made it to

Bodine's strong point, it was already clear that the resistance was falling back, building by building, faced with overwhelming military ordinance.

An armoured cavalry unit invested Les Vedettes, securing the Pont Neuf, and Dassault Rafale fighters strafed low over the Pantheon in a show of strength. Bodine and Bellew were of one mind. They gathered their unit leaders and gave the order to disperse. Under cover of nightfall word went out to scatter. Protected by covering fire, Luc and his commandos slipped over the Pont D'Austerlitz and melted away amongst the sympathetic population of Popincourt. By first light the sulphurous breath of a violent night still hung over the city. At first people stayed indoors. Through their broken windows they watched drunken stragglers wander about, shooting wildly into the air. Before mid morning hunger lured them out, trading eggs for matches, money for sugar and fresh bread. Exchanging stories of what they had seen and heard catalysed a murmur of anger amongst the inhabitants. A few well-meaning ring leaders called the community to action and, emerging from the side streets, ordinary citizens began to wind down the Rue de Charonne. First one hundred, then five hundred, building into thousands as they stood on the Place de la Bastille. They were in a sombre mood; they sang the 'Marseillaise'; some were accompanied by their children. Like a bubbling river, they overflowed the avenues and the sidewalks, overwhelming one police checkpoint after another, waving their tricolors and calling for 'Freedom' and 'Justice,' until a sudden dry flat stutter of machine gun fire opened up on them. Then some other Europol soldiers followed suit, firing off whole clips into the passing crowd at point blank range.

People stampeded, dragging blood-splattered bodies with them in all directions. Others threw themselves prostrate on the street or hunkered in doorways or behind kiosks and cars. A pregnant woman was shot in the abdomen and lay writhing in pain. Down the street, another woman was screaming hysterically, clutching at her face while stretcher-bearers ducked and weaved as they ran to aid the injured. One Europol officer strode up to a man who was holding onto his shattered knee cap by the kerbside, with a home-made placard on the ground next to him declaring France for the French. The officer took aim and fired directly into his face.

'There is a curfew,' announced an automated voice from the security forces megaphones strapped to the roofs of their cars and to the sides of helicopters, like angry metallic wasps, buzzing low over the city. 'Citizens are advised to stay indoors until order is restored!'

Having cleared the marchers off the street, the CRS began breaking down doors, smashing TV sets, and forcing women to disrobe for body searches. They hauled all the men of fighting age into commandeered transits, shipping them out to emergency internment camps beyond the city. Some police units deliberately drove through Val-d'Oise and Clichy-sous-Bois, pushing the odd resister out of the back of their vans into the jeering neighbourhoods were they were swiftly necklaced with burning tyres or stoned in full view of the authorities.

*

Arnaud Bellew stood on the speaker's platform wearing a black leather jacket, his hands moving slowly in the glow of a yellow spotlight shining from above, his eyes covered in dark shadows, his voice close to breaking.

'They think they've broken us . . . They think by taking away the alto they can silence a choir . . . Well they're wrong, our song gets louder and louder, it is echoing from north to south and east to west . . . We are like the hydra, strike in one place and we grow in another . . . Even now our comrades all the way from Galway in the west to the Urals in the east are joining us . . . you see our heart beats beyond our boundaries, it beats in the sun and the snow, across space and time, it flows with our soul, through rivers and forests, from the tops of mountains to the widest sea . . . It can never be silenced, not while we will it . . . '

Afterwards, Bardet's funeral cortege weaved through a rain soaked Belleville. Thousands of mourners followed the hearse. Luc walked in front of a small group of men who formed an honour guard for the vast procession, which for the first part of the journey was orderly and respectful. There were no drum bands or flags. The atmosphere was subdued. Police lined the streets in an effort to show authority rather than respect. All was quiet until the ceremony reached Père Lachaise where a marauding rabble had gathered to stone the coffin and the car bearing it, trying to stop the procession getting into the cemetery.

For nearly two hours the CRS failed to force passage through the surging mass before the cemetery's wrought iron gates. It later transpired that no one had ordered the local constabulary to allow the mob to disrupt the event. Ambulances came and went ferrying the fallen to hospital. Appeals to disperse were ignored until a French commandant ordered his men to get set to fire. Then, as his squad readied their guns, he strode out in full view of the protestors and ordered them to leave the vicinity or face the consequences.

No one was paying attention, they continued to hurl missiles and shout liberal abuse, convinced of their moral superiority and invincibility. Then ten men stepped forward, kneeling on the road, raising their guns to take aim. The first salvo took the protesters by surprise, some falling in shock as reality dawned on them. Others turned tail and made for cover in the trees of Rue de la Cloche.

Later, the officer who had cleared the path to the gates was seized and put on trial for authorising an act of genocide. After a brief hearing, presided over by one of Ben Hassi's cohorts, he was sentenced and killed *halal* style, a blade slicing his throat and his body bled before being returned to his family.

At Bardet's internment, Franck Bodine stood on the mound of brown soil in an attempt to gain the attention of the mass of cold wet bodies.

'Today we bury not just a man but a symbol,' he proclaimed, raising his right arm, 'our eternal fight goes on!'

Older heads shook. There was some heckling from the more conservative elements in the crowd who wanted to negotiate after the short, sharp lesson the Eurabic authorities had taught them.

Bodine waved their complaints away.

'Too many have already died to turn back now!' He sounded bitter and angry as the honour guard raised pistols over the coffin and fired a volley into the grey sky. Then he added, 'This struggle is only just beginning.' Afterwards, Sabine fought through the fracturing crowd carrying bedraggled banners from the graveside. Bodine and Bellew were talking to Luc conspiratorially. Later, she sat at a small run-down restaurant table, close to tears, waiting for all three to join her.

'What's wrong with these people?' she asked as they pulled up chairs and ordered whatever was left on the menu.

'Fear,' Bellew said, 'They are Ousset's children wracked by Catholic guilt. Look what they've just witnessed. No one could fail to be intimidated!'

'And that was exactly what was intended,' Luc retorted.

'Precisely,' Bodine spat, 'And now we fight fire with fire.'

After a long discussion the militants agreed on the following statement which Sabine, pulling out a pen from her bag, began to write down before it was relayed to their circle of allies on the Quai de L'Horloge and then sent to a pre-agreed list of media outlets.

*

DECLARATION OF WAR

The chronic cultural crisis that scars our society and the resulting political instability has led to the current upsurge in civil dissidence and the wanton murder of French citizens. It is clear that the present government will either continue to ignore the justified anger of our people, or will, as is more likely, side further with groups that seek to increase the severity of oppressive and tyrannical legislation.

Given that no other means are open to us we declare the commencement of revolutionary action. We will fight what we recognise as 'dictatorship.' Accusations that our urban or rural guerrilla units are criminal will be contested. They are in fact radical and green, in the sense that we fight for the re-balancing of the human eco-system that is under threat and neglected by politicians, priests, and administrators the length and breadth of this land. We will stop at nothing to achieve our goal.

LA SEMAINE SANGLANTE

We want it to be understood that the force we represent is an implacable enemy of this system that dominates and demoralizes our daily existence. Our targets will be economic and political.

STATEMENT ENDS.

*

Press Cuttings Bureaux :

Perigueux. Clerical officer maimed by parcel bomb.

Place de la Madeleine. Two men of Yemeni origin gunned down in a drive-by shooting.

Cannes. Attempted arson on a yacht registered in Tel Aviv.

Aubagne. Police station destroyed in motor attack; 11 killed, 23 injured.

Hyeres. Communist mayor wounded by man wielding a knife.

Marseilles. Street rioting leaves 3 dead and 52 with serious wounds.

Loctudy. Boat seized off Breton coast carrying shipment of firearms from Cornwall.

Alsace (location undisclosed). President's country estate suffers graffiti attack.

Larnaca. Three French nationals detained by request of Interpol.

Paris. Charles de Gaulle airport closed due to bomb threat.

Marignane. Student activist loses hand whilst attempting to detonate roadside bomb.

Lyon. Leftist street march comes under fire from unknown perpetrators.

Toulouse. Car bomb causes 20,000,000 euros' worth of damage to a retail centre.

A nationwide manhunt for over 200 named individuals begins. The list includes university professors, writers, shopkeepers, policemen, and various unemployed personages from 17 to 73. Over 40 women, several married with young children are known to be on the run . . .

*

'Stop there,' Sabine said pointing from the back seat. She had a mobile clamped tight to the side of her head, eyes wide. 'Luc says he just came out of the apartment.'

Her driver, André from the leafleting exploit, swivelled his black leather gloves on the steering wheel, aiming for the kerb.

'Dirty bastard,' he snorted, 'He's been fucking her all the time we've been driving around out here.'

André specialised in get-aways, aiding resistance fighters to escape after they had robbed banks or 'hit' targets around the city. They had been circling Chaillot in a stolen Peugeot for an hour, windscreen wipers sweeping aside the falling rain like a nosey neighbour peeking out from behind gauze curtains. The yellow repetitious glare of the garish shop windows along Rue Copernic stared back at them as they slowed down, the mesmeric backlighting of neon bulbs cooling in the wet of the evening. André stopped the engine, an orange streetlight just marginally tresspassing the surrounding cloak of darkness. Sabine, who had sat in moody silence all the way from Beauvais was suddenly stirred into action.

'Move there a little,' she pointed, 'That light will give us away!' André fired the ignition, the car slurred sluggishly into action.

'We should have got a better car,' he moaned as they rolled forward, the hubcap grating on an open manhole cover until they were hidden under a small tree. They were at the junction of the Rue Paul Valery and the Rue Lauriston, just off the Avenue Kleber. André looked in the rear view mirrow to scan for police or traffic wardens. Sabine was rummaging in her looped leather handbag, as if searching for some lipstick or sunglasses, until her fingers closed on the cold metal of the revolver. Her driver waited nervously, perspiring while she slipped open the chamber, swivelling it anti-clockwise, carefully loading the shells one by one from a small box of waxed cardboard. Bodine had supplied the bullets at their new operation centre in the north of the city.

'Execute that lying rat with extreme prejudice,' he had said, having just seen a Canal Plus documentary libelling one of the resistance leaders, alleging involvement in a paedophile ring.

*

André watched as Sabine rolled the silver tipped shells in her palm, counting to six carefully, kissing the last one with a mischievous smile.

'For luck,' she said, conscious of her partner's agitation.

'Just do it!' he said.

Sabine opened the door and proceeded to turn her face this way and that, trying to chase her target to ground. People were casually drifting by, browsing the *chic* stores, gossiping *en route* to a cinema or a restaurant down Rue Boissiere.

André caught sight of Sabine's heavily mascaraed eyes prowling like a panther, waiting for its prey to emerge. She shifted on the seat, twisting her coat about her and pulling back the hammer. They both heard the catch click. Eventually, the bulky media magnate emerged from rippling rays of light. She raised the gun, levelling it at the man.

'Christ,' she's with him, André warned, 'You can't!'

Ignoring his objections, Sabine aligned the sight with her subject's head, aiming directly at Charles Ackmann's fat mouth. Her finger pressed on the trigger and then, with two quick flicks of her wrist, she let him have it. The Smith & Wesson barked and threw the fat man backwards, arms flailing, smashing through a plate glass window. A spume of hot blood and faecal matter jetted over the display of lycra-covered mannequins in the shop front display and some fragments of his shattered skull, hair still attached, scratched across the lips of the blonde woman walking at his side.

Before André could stop her, Sabine was out the door, body low to the ground, gun stretched out in front of her, leaving a trail of cordite in her wake. With a sudden fluid heave André was sick over himself, his groin covering in regurgitated chicken. Sabine approached Ackmann slowly; he was slumped over jagged glass, his clotted Armani coat now no more than a death shroud. Alarms were whirring, lights flashing as if it were a smash-and-grab raid. She moved in close, saw a stream of splashed blood spotted over the display—toppled dummies, contorted torsos strewn with holes. The man's face was unrecognisable, a pulp of smashed crimson cartilage and jagged bone bubbling with trickling raindrops. His female companion's long shapely legs were shaking with shock. She was screaming hysterically and waving her hands in front of her face, trying to spit out the taste of her lover's viscera. Sabine turned and stood, quite deliberately targeting her weapon on the girl's vagina.

'Hi sister,' she hissed, 'I see you like circumcised cock!'

The sweep of car headlights framed them dramatically against the flashing shop façade and falling rain: Sabine, in a long dark coat and huge gold earrings, strands of hair falling loosely about her face, arm outstretched, gun pointing accusingly; her adversary, fresh from a tryst with her dead lover, begging for her life, pleading pitifully for Sabine not to shoot. In the background, passers-by were scattering as the executioner took aim. At the first attempt the revolver misfired. Sabine straightened up, lifting the gun a second time. Again the hammer fell without effect. The blonde's bladder gave way.

'You realise, three times and I'll have to let you go,' Sabine mocked, raising the stakes for all to hear before two further shots cracked out loudly in the dampness.

The blonde's aquiline body was blown into the gutter behind the stolen Peugeot. Only a red high-heel shoe remained where she had stood. Droplets of warm yellow urine glistened on patent leather.

Sabine ran back to the car. 'Go, go, go . . . !'

*

Official response of the Minister of Interior Justice, his excellency, Said Ben Hassi to the recent communication(s) received through various media sources relating to attempts to ferment public disorder:

The state recognises the threat to its citizens from unprovoked acts of terrorism by radical groups in these turbulent times. Let it be understood that such illegal behaviour and murders like that of Monsieur Ackmann, Chief Executive of Trans Media global will be met head on by the full force of the police and security services. We will leave no stone unturned in pursuit of the perpetrators of indiscriminate violence. From what we know of the group or groups responsible for these random activities and the subsequent communications, it is clear they are untrained, leaderless and insignificant in terms of numbers. It is also unclear as to their purpose and therefore their demands will not be acknowledged in the sense that they designate themselves as 'freedom fighters.' We are free. Our Eurabic society is stable and diverse. Recent aberrations are merely growing pains in the long journey towards true equality. It is they, the so-called resistance, who are unstable and trying to tarnish all our hopes and ambitions for a better future. We will treat them as criminals and make known at all times the collateral damage their mafia actions inflict upon innocent people in the hope that this will negate any misguided support they seek to gain among the populace.

Issued 9.30 am Wednesday 17th November.

En vacance

ach morning, whilst the whole town got on with the day, Sabine lay closed off behind the wooden shutters of the apartment listening to the sound of drilling and the chipping of steel tools on the road outside. When she was in the mood she would stand with a well-thumbed copy of Gentile's collected works, looking at the boats moored by the bridge, rippling blue rolling out, swirling around the stone footings. The air sparkled in the fresh Umbrian sunlight. Later, she would join the customers eating ice cream and listen to live amateur opera in the plaza.

Most days, the cell would wake simultaneously and laze in their underwear in the small complex of rooms they had rented under a false name. Few words were spoken as they sat around the kitchen table busying themselves with their ordnance, priming munitions and polishing weaponry. One morning, lying in bed, Sabine pulled a Beretta from under the pillow and stroked its cold barrel along her soft thigh. She could hear Luc in the shower. The steady trickle of water in the next room made a soothing accompaniment, and reaching down between her legs, she closed her eyes and pleasured herself.

Around noon she kicked off the sheets, prised her body from under the duvet. A narrow bathroom window gave out on a courtyard and Sabine, knickers around her ankles, sat peeing whilst Luc stood in front of the mirror in a white vest shaving. Since their arrival they had established a well-ordered routine, split between daylight and nocturnal activities. Sabine would stretch before her yoga, others would sit and read novels by d'Annunzio and tracts by Codreanu, heads tilted, inhaling deeply on Italian MS cigarettes. Around six they would gather on the balcony, play cards and listen to each others' idealistic dreams while rolling joints and comparing notes about the street map on a circular metal table. Luc settled in his chair, behind him the vast dome of the basilica set against the burnt ochre sunset. He would talk about their mission and run his finger along the confluence of boulevards and parks as they unfolded on paper in front of them.

Before going out on reconnaissance missions Sabine and Luc would sometimes stand side by side on the balcony while the rest of the team dressed and stare out over the water in meditative silence. The large church across the narrow channel was a backlit silhouette. Small boats slipped over the river calling to each other in the demi-blue twilight. The two would nod to each other before gathering their things, each privately acknowledging the primary importance of the other to the operation.

'Ready?' Luc would say, moving towards the sitting room.

Sabine would step inside, closing the glass door on the balcony behind her. He would always cover their backs, taking the key from the telephone table, locking the door, and following the others down the unlit staircase, tucking a handgun inside his shirt.

Throughout the town, at all the junctions of major streets and the busiest squares, were small cylindrical kiosks, which sold newspapers and magazines in a thousand languages. Pedestrians stopped to buy cigarettes, passing their notes through an arrow slit hatch, seeing only a brown hand and the vendor's suspicious eyes glaring out from the darkness within.

Sabine walked several metres ahead, moving as though measuring out a distance. Behind her the others carried cloth bags and leather satchels stretched across their shoulders. Moving up a narrow passageway they came upon a large, dimly-lit square with a war memorial at its centre. They crossed and filtered themselves through the crowds milling about streets full of shops selling dishwashers, televisions, and furniture. They navigated the avenues and plunged into dark side alleys. Luc found himself looking at Sabine's back, her shoulder blades rose and fell in sync with her stride, her hair gathered tightly at the back of her head by a butterfly clasp, pony-tail swinging to and fro. The fluorescent streetlights bleached out her defining characteristics until she became part shadow once more, an elfin apparition of a pagan banshee stepping out of a poem by Yeats.

They came to a junction where the street divided. On the corner stood an imposing semi-derelict building, a row of stone statuary staring down on them from rusting balconies and high arched windows. The entrance was barred by a corrugated tin fence, which was covered in fly-posters supporting One World groups and feminist covens.

'I see our lesbian friends are better organised around here,' Luc said.

'More radical too,' Sabine confirmed translating one of the pink stickers, 'It's no wonder most Italian men live with their mothers!'

Luc stepped back onto the kerb, frowning, his head moving from side to side comparing the two street names to the folded map in his hands.

'Which way now?' Sabine said.

'I'm not sure.'

He moved to get a better view of the street to his right. Sabine stood looking, feet apart, the others standing, awaiting orders.

'That is the fountain there on your map,' she said, 'So we go left!'

They followed behind her at a precise pace, their footsteps quickening, shoes resounding noisily on the cobbles as they came up to the ancient drinking fountain. Luc stepped up to the worn bowl lowering his head to the tarnished brass faucet.

'Christ,' he said drawing back from the tumbling water, 'It tastes like Chinese pussy . . . !'

Everyone laughed.

'Yeah, like you'd know!' Sabine said.

When they moved on, they saw in the distance a figure emerge out of the glow of a streetlight, coming towards them.

'Are you French tourists?' the stranger said.

'Yes!' Luc confirmed.

'I am Paulo, your guide,' came the reply. 'Please follow me and I will help with all your arrangements.'

*

John Costello came to town in a glaze of lemon light. The hot summer afternoon was well advanced as he stepped off the bus, sports bag in hand, pale Panama hat cocked at a jaunty angle. Arrangements for carnival were in their last stages. A small square at the centre of a tight cobweb of cobbled streets was to be the epicentre of festivities. Jutting balconies overlooked turn-of-the century façades lined with cafés and exclusive boutiques, the pavements shaded by clay-tiled rooftops and twisting pink wisteria. People walked across the open space as if blissfully unaware that on every other day of the year this urban sprawl was filled with bumper-to-bumper traffic and honking horns, trucks passing south to the coast. Most of the proprietors whose shops opened up onto the square had laid out wooden stalls in front of their big glass display windows in anticipation of brisk trade. Several workmen in blue overhauls were on top of ladders, their hands pulling on wires stretching coloured bunting across the street. Every window ledge was awash with flowers. At the far end of the concourse, standing tall behind a cascading silver fountain, the sandstone government building was bedecked with a myriad of small triangular fluttering flags. On the plaza there was a gaudily coloured fairground, a roundabout and rowboats swinging gently on creaking chains.

He checked in to his hotel, threw his luggage on the bed, unpacked his hand gun and walked straight back out onto the street. As he waited outside, a black stretch limousine glided effortlessly by, tinted windows shielding the occupants. The car stopped in a nearby side street close to the large red, canopied entrance to the city's best hotel. The King George V was the former summer residence of some Italian prince, elegant, baroque and with that north-

ern Italian hint of styled luxury that few other cul-
tures can conceive, let alone readily display or carry
off with such effect. The car doors swung open and
dark-suited men stepped onto shimmering tarmac,
looking about from behind Raybans. Taking orders
from wire earpieces, they ushered the hunched figure of the regional councillor, Bruno Gallo, hobbling
on a cane, through the revolving glass panels into
the ostentatious air-conditioned foyer.

Costello waited and watched until they were all
inside, knowing there was a clandestine VIP meeting scheduled in the next few days, then walked in
the opposite direction, mindlessly wandering until
he was lost in a forest of red, white, and green café
canopies squared off by a façade of cathedral colon-
nades. Although his orders were to find them and
report back to his masters in the Elysées, Costello
guessed that contact would result in a shoot out.
Above him the red brick clock tower was smothered
in a grey flutter of strutting, excreting, and nodding
pigeons. Sitting down to order an espresso, he tried
to anticipate Sabine and Luc's next move. He sat
staring at the brown slops in the diminutive cup in
front of him. The French had supplied him with a
mass of confidential material, some of a very sensitive nature. He doubted Fouvier's optimism that
Sabine and her group were just getting out of France
until the 'heat' went off them. Costello was sure they
were planning something. The apparently secret
meeting in the King George V was far too auspicious
to be a coincidence and there had been chatter of
Franco-Italian resistance cooperation for some
months. He twisted his head and saw a couple
struggling to entertain a young child amid the ash-
trays and empty cups. The fleshy little creature was
wearing a blue hat and a sailor's bibby. Just for a
second he wondered how different things might

have been if Sabine had a baby. And at that moment his mobile phone rang.

'Costello here . . . no sign as yet, no idea . . . but I know they are here.'

'We have just intercepted intel from an Italian informant that they will be in receipt of arms and explosives from local agitators!' Fouvier's voice was anxious. 'Our source is very reliable. I think I may have been wrong about them taking a vacation. I simply cannot afford a diplomatic incident . . . Kill her if necessary' the Inspecteur's voice trailed off.

Later, when he picked up more calls from Bruyere all he could say was that if they had travelled this far then he was expecting something big but could not be sure.

'I have a gut instinct,' he kept saying before hanging up. The thought of holding a gun to Sabine's face stuck in his mind. Would he shoot he asked himself? Costello waved a hand at the waiter who swooped towards him like a falcon on a dive. The man, a large fellow with a thin goatee beard and gold-rimmed spectacles inclined towards him.

'Check please,' the special services man asked and showing him a photograph of Sabine asked discreetly 'Have you seen my daughter? She's got a drug problem, you know?'

The waiter shook his head.

'*Bella ragazza!*' he said, 'I would remember her!'

Later, he followed his nose, walking in the blue grey light bouncing off block granite. Somewhere, a high-pitched bell peeled over the rooftops.

When he returned to the hotel, the festivities were just beginning. Costello's fingers ran tensely over the metal butt of his weapon. He caught his first sight of Sabine as she stood silently by a display of hats in a leather store. She was wearing a blue dress and her hair hung straight and long. She was like a dark raven in the midst of the revellers, aloof and distant, her beady eyes searching the crowds. As he walked across the square towards his objective, she moved on and lost herself in the parades. He waited by a leather shop, hoping to catch sight of her again, but failed. After a few minutes, he changed position, standing at the entrance to a narrow curved alley that ran in a gradual descending pattern of worn rutted steps to the east and then the south east before being carried away over the humped back of an old stone bridge.

Costello decided to take a chance and followed the curve of the street down to the waterfront. He nonchalantly sauntered about in front of weather beaten houses looking for her among the fish stalls and the hawkers trying to sell boat trips to tourists. When he admitted to himself he had lost her he sat down at the quay's edge and breathed in the smell of dead fish. Before him a low wall ran off into the distance. His eyes could make out the cupolas of catholic churches and the long fingers of minarets poking the sky. The jetty was deserted but he walked to the end just to see if she could have made off by water.

*

He knew she and Luc were elusive and deadly. London had briefed him that there were at least three others, all personally trained by Franck Bodine, accompanying her when she crossed the border. The signs were ominous. An old leather-faced fisherman tried to engage him in conversation but he waved him off. Returning to his room, he sat in silence for an hour cleaning his gun and then ordered more coffee. Standing on the wrought-iron balcony, his eyes surfed the scene below, trying to pick out faces, signals for what might transpire. Around five, he went back out into the square and came upon her dark profile, once again, set against the side of a white van transporting fairground equipment. Sabine was walking at right angles to his sightlines, staring thoughtfully at the ground. He watched her until she reached the steps outside the government buildings and slowly began to ascend them, pushing through the crowds of families, eating candyfloss and ice cream, excitedly streaming up and down. At the top she turned and faced back towards him. Their eyes met across the square, gazing at one another. He thought he detected recognition and opted for a decisive move. He walked on and reaching the bottom of the steps, his fingers slipped inside his jacket pocket, searching for his weapon. Sabine turned and disappeared into a shaded portico. He went up to where she had been standing and lingered for a moment, trying to melt into the multitude milling about before the building. Behind him there was a sudden flash of light. The blowback threw him forward onto his hands and face. He heard the delayed sound of a percussive explosion and a scream, then the report of a revolver letting loose in panic and the flurry of leather shoes on pavings. He did not dare to get up and turn around. For a couple of minutes the square was filled with dense dust and fizzling smoke. When the cloud of debris cleared, someone finally thought to switch off the Wurlitzer music that kept repeating on a loop, mocking the shrill sound of a mother's sobbing. He swivelled around almost reluctantly, and saw a child's severed limbs tangled in the road, blood pooling at the stumps.

The diversion had worked because Luc Dubois and the rest of the cell had simultaneously entered the King George V hotel, gunning down the flustered dark-suited men in Raybans gathered around reception, and taking hostage Bruno Gallo, the old regional counsellor, and Abdul Aleem Dajani, the *Chargé d'Affaires* of the United League of Muslim Nations. Luc's squad had then collected together all the evidence spread out on the mahogany meeting table for the proposed partition of Italy into the European north and the Arabic south along a line from Pescara to Fiumicino.

After seizing the traitors and conveying them to a safehouse, where they would film and broadcast their confessions on the internet, Luc had insisted on a prisoner exchange at a pass in the Tyrol before joining Sabine in Vienna, where they would live amongst sympathisers for three months, ghosting back over the French border at Mulhouse once it was safe.

*

COMMUNIQUE NO 1

> We refuse to submit to genocide regardless of whatever form it chooses to take. This was France, it remains France, and it will always be France. There will be no compromise with our people's posterity!

*

Taking the best from their predecessors, like the Irish Republican Army and the Red Army Faction, the Resistance continued to strike at the heart of the Eurabic state in small commando units, organised on the principle of phantom cells, conducting a war of the flea upon the system. Their operatives worked alone or in pairs. The government were constantly denied the opportunity to bring the full force of the army and its covert intelligence apparatus against them and thus were rarely in a position to neutralise any significant portion of the movement . . .'

*

COMMUNIQUE NO 2

> We are political soldiers. Our agenda is to over-throw the tyrannous imposition of the Eurabic state . . . There will be no 'pause' button . . .

*

The Resistance attacked on multiple and diverse fronts. Anticipating that the initial media frenzy would soon give way to a news 'blackout' they relied on their own media. Mindful of Yves Godard's model of network analysis, which had proven effective in breaking the FLN during the liberation campaign in Algeria, they stuck to Louis Beam's strategy of 'leaderless resistance'.

Some individuals only engaged in single acts of terrorism, which made them difficult to identify and convict. More highly skilled political soldiers submerged themselves in a myriad of safehouse systems, not unlike the Werewolf network Himmler envisaged as the German Reich was rolled back to its Berlin hub.

PART THREE

The Trial

Late in the morning she was taken by Sebastian Bruyere to the examining magistrate's office. The windows were thrown open and the room was filled with natural light. The Eurabists had changed the face of the city. Hundreds of statues had been removed and in the distance the sound of the *muezzins* calling *adhan* could be heard floating over the rooftops.

'This is D'Orlac,' Bruyere said introducing his charge to the wizened old man sitting behind the large wooden desk. So this mere girl was the cause of such mayhem, the symbolic witch Ben Hassi wanted to make an example of? The magistrate, Isaac Chelouche, signalled for her to join him. After a short silence, while he looked her up and down as if studying some kind of strange exotic insect, he leaned forward, staring deep into her eyes.

'Why?' he asked, 'why have you become entangled in such things?'

'What things?' Sabine's top lip was buttoned tight like a convent girl's gymslip. Chelouche's wrinkles danced with irritation.

'Evasion will not help you,' he said coldly, 'Your case interests government at the highest levels. I am granting the Surete's request for an unlimited period of further questioning prior to charges being brought and assigning you a state lawyer as required by law.'

'I can speak for myself!' Chelouche's lizard-like tongue uncoiled its contempt.

'Mademoiselle, I will afford you no opportunity to espouse your hateful philosophy. The new Eurabic state will not indulge such ramblings, or any other nonsense for that matter which is not directly linked to the case in hand. Do you understand me?' In the moments that followed his unequivocal statement the magistrate kept his ever narrowing eyes focussed on her. Finally, thrusting his notebook on the desk, he repeated, 'Do you understand me?'

'Oh, I fully understand you!'

'Good,' he said aggressively, 'Your France is dead, gone forever, *finis!*' Then dismissing her, he turned once more to the metallic menorah on the shrine in the corner of his office and began the mumbling and nodding supplications of his tribe.

*

Next day a small plump lawyer came to her cell. The shutters opened on a dapper middle-aged man with grey receding hair and yellow teeth.

'Bonjour,' he said, 'My name's Rene Chambroux, I am here to represent you,' After the usual preliminary introductions he sat on the edge of her bed, patting his brown leather briefcase with a pair of porcine hands. 'You know,' he said, 'in all seriousness, I think this is a very difficult case.' He looked up hoping to elicit some kind of acknowledgement from her. Sabine stood stone-faced, utterly disconcerting him. Chambroux shuffled on the bed-cover. 'Do you think we can claim some form of mental disorder?' Her eyes widened with surprise. 'Normally I don't like to suggest such a thing but you really need to understand the severity of your situation. The authorities will press for the full penalty of the law!'

'I know,' she murmured.

'Then you are aware of the potential consequences?' He looked away, pained to talk of the guillotine in front of such a young woman.

'I am a soldier,' she replied, 'I accept the consequences of war.'

'But there is no war!' he said.

'You don't think so?'

'Some civil adjustments, maybe, I know they are painful but time will heal . . . '

She cut him dead: 'It is war in all but name.'

Chambroux tried to shift the discourse. 'Do you feel any regret for the things you have done?'

'*Non*, I acted out of natural and healthy instincts.'

'But people have died.'

'So?'

'Innocent people!'

'True, there has been unintended collateral damage, but that is inevitable. Think of the thousands of our people who have lost their liberty or their lives because of this *putsch*!'

The lawyer shook his head, fingers scratching at his jaw. 'There was a legally signed treaty of Franco-Islamic federation and clauses to ensure democratic processes, what more can we hope for?'

Sabine threw back her hair, bayonet eyes staring. 'A free France without columns of *Mujahidin* marching past the *Arc de Triomphe*.'

The man facing her tut-tutted. 'You must promise me not to repeat such racist things in front of the Public Prosecutor. My job is difficult enough. You'd be signing your own death sentence!'

'You don't think it is already fixed?'

'This is France!' the legal counsel said, 'We live under the rule of law!'

'This is not France; this is an abomination!'

'This is France!' Chambroux insisted.

Sabine smiled. 'We all know the politically correct platitudes and the evil opinions that we are not supposed to speak. They've made automatons and zombies of us all. The sheep do what is expected of them, what is acceptable and how to fulfil their designated roles.'

'*Who* expects?' said Chambroux.

'The people who pay your wages.' Chambroux went to defend himself but her hand shot out, 'They are absolutist. They seek to end all opposition. From them there can be no safe havens. There are asylums and prison camps for people who step out of line. They have re-education centres, don't they? And I bet your children have a very selective curriculum.'

'Who, *who*?' Chambroux's hands beat down on the flat leather face before him.

'Saint-Just said *no one can rule guiltlessly*. There are millions of Isaac Chelouche's type infesting the whole structure of our government. It's the same in the United States. Who do you think pulls their strings?'

The lawyer stood, offended she would quote Saint-Just at him.

'And statements like that could end matters once and for all,' he said turning on his heels rapping on the metal door and asking to be released, '*Au revoir!*'

*

They clamped the cuffs on her wrists and led her down the hall. Both Bruyere and Fouvier supervised the transit. Costello stood in silence. The captive and he exchanged a respectful nod.

'Next time,' Sabine smiled confidently.

As the door was opened onto the street, the roar of the waiting crowd filled the vacuum in the narrow entrance. A cordon of police surrounded a convoy ready to take her to the courtroom. Beyond the police lines were a myriad of hate-filled faces, throwing excrement and chanting, 'One World, One People!' As Sabine stepped through the door and they got their first sight of her the protesters grew even louder, reaching fever pitch as she became fully visible. The masses bussed in from Bondy and Seine-Saint-Denis pushed and strained against the thin blue line of gendarmes who had linked arms to form a human chain.

'Whore!' She heard them call, 'Slut!'

Then she felt salty spittle splash her face and bare legs. A young man in matted blonde dreadlocks threw aside his bongo drums and tried to lunge for her but was brought down short by a police truncheon. Sabine stumbled on the last step as a bright light caught her attention. A tricolor was being torched by a tight knot of dancing Burundians. Cameras were flashing like the Cannes film festival as she was made to stand in front of the armoured car, waiting for them to open up and load her in, eyes flaring with defiance.

They pushed her through a crack in the armoured plated doors in the glare of the live TV feeds. Dwarfed by the two guards, she looked aghast at the burning flag and the prancing jackals. Bruyere watched for Fouvier's instruction and, receiving a nod of confirmation, slapped the side of the armoured vehicle, sending it off into seething streets. Sirens screamed and the motorcade rolled slowly down the route d'Orleans. Outside, beyond the tinted windscreen and the air-tight protection, manic screams and tin drums played all along the route. Bystanders on the pavement made lewd gestures as the convoy passed by the Porte d'Orleans, making for the Luxembourg Gardens and the Boulevard Saint-Michel. Now Sabine felt on familiar territory, close to the Latin Quarter, wheels running parallel to the lapping brown Seine, the tide drawn inevitably towards the Quai de L'Horloge. There, dismounting from the transport, she was pulled along a labyrinth of stairways and stared at in the hallways by back office staff who had never seen a monster before. She played along by growling, sending them rushing back to their desks.

The assize court was already frothing with the press and media. Hand-picked members of the public from the new French diaspora sat in a gallery looking down into the cold cavernous civic forum where the trial was about to take place. There was not an empty seat in the house. Famous faces were sprinkled liberally in the crowd. There was Marcel Ayme the existentialist philosopher, Thomas Cavanna, the leader of the socialist bloc and various editors and commentators from magazines and news forums, all looking forward to guffawing and barking their well orchestrated self-righteous condemnation at the accused.

Around 1300 hours Sabine was ushered into the courtroom via a side door that was guarded by two of Ben Hassi's Zouave soldiers in full ceremonial robes, brown hands gripping tight the pommels of curved scimitars. A single female gendarme in a sweaty blue shirt sat next to her in the raised wooden dock for all to see. President of the court, Monsieur Jacques-Alain de Sedouy, an owl of a man sitting under a melange of flags representing the new hybrid France, commenced proceedings.

'This court is now in session,' he said to all and then turning towards the dock, 'Miss Sabine D'Orlac . . . ,' his voice strained but dignified, 'You are currently unemployed and of no fixed address, is that correct?'

'Yes, Mr President,' Sabine answered, standing, coughing through a clenched fist, throat hoarse from cigarette smoke.

'Pass the defendant some water,' de Sedouy asked a court assistant and a jug and glass were brought to the dock.

'Merci,' Sabine swallowed hard.

'Miss D'Orlac, you must pay attention to the indictment you are about to hear. It is very important you comprehend the significance of the crimes of which you are accused and the potential severity of any sentence the court may find against you. Do you understand?'

'Mr President,' she replied 'I do not recognise the authority of this court to judge any of my past activities or my political opinions.'

'Miss D'Orlac, I am only too aware of your very independent and unique views regarding the legitimacy of the current legislature and must advise you that in the absence of any other civil authority in this country you are subject to the one that I represent here today and will answer the charges brought before this court I preside over . . . '

Sabine took another long drink and ran a hand through her hair. 'My position is clear,' she said, 'I am a prisoner of war and you, Sir, represent a government of occupation.'

'Mr Darnand, read the indictment please,' the President continued, brushing aside the accused's remark as if absurd. The crowd in the gallery bristled with intemperate anger and raked the courtroom with offended bug eyes. A small man in a black suit, a tight white collar, and long fluorescent yellow tie began in a high pitched, almost whining voice. 'The indictment reads as follows,' a slight nervous pause for breath, then, 'That you did conduct acts of terrorism in this and other states; that you were and are a member of a proscribed criminal organisation; that you hold views that are illegal under the current law codes; that you have distributed literature that has inflamed public passions and incited others to violence against individuals and the state . . .'

'Miss D'Orlac,' the Court President interjected, 'each of these charges carries a number of lesser-affiliated witness summons, all of which are listed in the papers circulated to your counsel. I now ask you how you plead to these and all the other accusations noted in the deposition.'

Sabine, still standing, lifted her shackles, metal glinting under the spotlights for all to see. 'Monsieur, I deny the right of this illegitimate sultanate to judge me. I cannot possibly receive a fair trial when the juror's,' her head turning to the potpourri of men and women sitting to her left, 'many of whom are not even French citizens, have no doubt been pre-selected by this despotic system.'

'I require a simple guilty or not guilty plea!' de Sedouy said.

'What is this? A kangaroo court? Or a lynching party?'

'Mr Chambroux,' the President said, turning to Sabine's defence lawyer, 'is it your client's plan to delay or obstruct this case?' I must warn you, if this is the intention, it will not mitigate the impending judgement.'

'Mr President,' Chambroux answered excitedly, 'My client is quite possibly suffering from post traumatic stress syndrome . . . '

'Mr President,' Sabine interrupted 'as you well know, this man is a court-appointed lawyer, he's been forced upon me and is quite possibly in league with the prosecution.'

'Miss D'Orlac, are you waving your right to counsel?'

'Yes!'

'Who will represent you?'

'I will represent myself,'

President Sedouy turned to the microphone to his right.

'Ladies and gentlemen, in the light of this development, I am recommending we adjourn proceedings for one hour.'

*

'Miss D'Orlac, I am in no doubt as to the dangerous views you hold. This however is not a trial to match that of Dreyfuss or even Robert Brasillach. Please stop your interruptions and allow the prosecutor to speak,' Sedouy said from his dais. Her opponent, the state prosecutor, pursed his fat lips to start again.

'And in relation to the lady's mental condition, and in response to the only contribution made by her counsel earlier, I can assure you that by all reasonable standards and criteria the accused is of sound mind and mentally agile. Her vigorous behaviour here today reveals her commitment to the cause that has brought her to this point. Ladies and gentlemen of the jury, what we are dealing with is a determined member of a terrorist cell hell-bent upon illegal activities that threaten the existence of order and respect within our inclusive and dare I say harmonious community.'

Sabine leapt to her feet.

'This is a show trial. You,' Sabine shouted incredulously, pointing at the prosecutor 'You are a state puppet! Who in their right mind would describe our broken society, in a time of near civil war, as politically harmonious? It is you not me that needs psychiatric analysis!'

'Miss D'Orlac,' if you persist behaving like this I may be obliged to remove you from the proceedings.'

'A mock trial in absentia,' she hissed, 'just like the USSR!'

'Please do not force my hand, I am only too aware that your objective is to use this trial as a platform to propagate your convictions and portray yourself as a martyr.'

'For every one you sentence now, ten will follow.'

'God spare us such a calamity!' de Sedouy rejoined.

The people in the courtroom were getting agitated now, increasingly frustrated that the President was giving her a platform.

'No airtime for the reactionary!' someone shouted in the gallery. 'Swift justice!' echoed back. Sabine was on her feet, shaking her chains.

'You wouldn't be saying such things if I wasn't cuffed!' A Zouave guard stepped forward, drawing his blade as he approached, the blue-shirted female gendarme pulled Sabine back down onto the bench seat.

'*Asseyez-vous!*'

'Enough!' Sedouy declared, 'I am closing this first day of the hearing with a clear warning, that should proceedings continue in this manner I will be forced to hold this tribunal in private session. Is that understood?,' his eyes flashed grey-green and steel hard like cold lightning bolts toward the young woman sitting in the dock and her detractors in the gallery. He wrapped down hard with his gavel, 'We re-convene tomorrow at 10 am sharp.'

*

The next day commenced with eye witness statements:

'She was about twenty-two or twenty-three, with a beautiful lithe body, every movement impregnated with casual sensuality. I watched her from behind, sitting at a wooden bench under the shade of a line of chestnut trees, sunlight flecking her pale cheek. A middle aged instructor, silver grey glittering in his hair, stood over her, glancing at a stop watch, counting down time every ten seconds . . . ' read the anonymous man from behind the curtain.

' . . . I saw her two little hands take apart the Kalashnikov's bolt and return spring, then reassemble it in the heat of the noon sun. Her bare arms exposed under the rolled up sleeves of an olive green tunic, her thighs jerking about in tight camouflaged fatigues. I can remember thinking she must have been doing this for ages to be so proficient, so drilled. When the instructor took a blindfold out of his pocket, I thought to myself she will never be able to do it, but she did not flinch. He waited patiently until she had laid all the oily parts back out on the cedar planks in front of her before fastening the black cloth like a tourniquet around her head and taking a few moments to spread the weapon's parts about the table top like a hunter might separate the desiccated innards of a deer. Then he stood back, took a deep breath and shouted for her to go, his gnarled thumb clicking the stopwatch to start . . .

"Length?" he barked. "Eight hundred and eighty millimetres." "Weight?" "Four point five kilograms" "Accuracy?" "Up to three hundred metres!" she replied. "Rounds per minute?" "Six hundred!"

'. . . Later I realised I must have fallen in love with her that day. She was like a woodland sprite, all puckering lips and big doleful eyes under a mop of dark brown hair pulled back in a ponytail. I noticed her slim waist, the green vest knotted at the navel. The insolent angle of her face when she sat cross-legged forking sausages from a mess tin. Everything she did seemed magical. I can remember how my head thumped with the first burst of AK-47 fire. Catching sight of her taking aim, legs apart, thin arms lifting her gun, hips swaying like she was dancing. Spent cartridges flying everywhere, whirring bullets shattering a plywood target before my eyes.'

> Pre-prepared Witness Statement.
> Marc Bergere.
> Concluded 11.30 am on Day 2 of the trial.

'She means nothing to me. I never heard of her . . . '

> Excerpt of recorded statement.
> Name: Etienne Levert

Age: 47
Occupation: Printer
Town: Angouleme
Charge: Distributing prohibited literature

'We were taught aggression and self-sufficiency by ex-army sympathisers. Our equipment and training was inferior to the state's, so we had to be imaginative and decisive. Food, fuel, and ammunition were the staples. This was followed by theoretical underpinning. We studied Hans Von Dach's *Total Resistance* and Carl Schmitt's *Theory of the Partisan*. We were hardened up with street fights and forced to be fast on our feet. All our focus was on blending in with the masses and doing nothing to stand out. The technical preparation was especially demanding. Basic chemistry and physics also helped in the making of pipe bombs, trip switches, and digital detonators. We could also patch ourselves up with a baseline knowledge of how to dress gunshot wounds and recuperation after injury. All the time it was about hit and run. I remember firing handguns like the Sig Sauer and the Glok for hours until our wrists hurt. Christ knows where they got all the bullets but there were boxes and boxes of them . . . '

Excerpt from written statement.
Name: Jan Picard
Age: 32
Occupation: Machine shop operative
Town: Arras
Charge: Conspiracy

'There were political lectures in the training camps in the woods around Montsegur. We would gather, still sweating from our exertions under the trees to drink water and lemon juice. There were huge banners that read 'In Paris as in Gaza Intifada' and 'Europe, Youth, Revolution.' Sometimes Franck Bodine or Luc Dubois would jump up on a stump in their military fatigues and harangue us about the sacrality of war. They would constantly refer to the ideals of the Spartans and the historical significance of Thermopylae. It was like an obsession with them. Sabine D'Orlac would sit at their feet like a starstruck pupil with a crush on the professor. Her fingers constantly toying with the safety catch on her gun.'

Name:Lucien Rebatet
Age: 25
Occupation: Taxi driver
Town: Saint-Flour
Charge: Armed robbery

'Yeah, I remember, a real nasty bitch!'

Name: Guy Croussy
Age:51
Occupation: Unemployed
Town: Bar-le-Duc
Charge: Murder

Breakout

Here they come!' the radio van blurted exult-
antly.

A TV reporter provided a running commen-
tary through the loudspeakers for Canal
Plus. Hundreds of heads bent their red goi-
tre faces over the cold railings, arms beating
like fitting epileptics. Socialist flags were unfurled
from windows, people gathered on balconies overlooking the street where green moon and crescent
banners were strung across the shop fronts.

'Viva El Ahmed!' everyone was shouting.

The air was alive with expectation. Talk went
around that they were only minutes away. Church
bells began to ring out in welcome all over Carpen-
tras. Everyone was saying 'Two minutes, just two
minutes away...' Men in dark suits with lumpy
pockets lined the route. Klaxons whirred and the
sound of clapping echoed like drum beats off the
walls. Two police motorbikes came around the
bend. Then the Presidential motorcade swept

through the freshly scrubbed streets, sirens wailing and a single African pennant fluttering on the black wing of a Bentley as it swung into view.

It was the 10th October, the anniversary of the battle of Tours, the *ma 'arakat balat ash-Shuhada*, as the Muslims named it. Today's embassy of reconciliation from Tangiers was meant to end centuries of enmity and finally bury the divisive legend of Charles Martel. Luc got the feeling that behind the tinted windows evil eyes surveyed their possessions. From his vantage point he lifted the M72 and aimed its smooth bore barrel at the car, pulling gently on the trigger, releasing the fin rocket into the road.

*

STATEMENT FROM THE COMMISSARIAT OF POLICE

We can confirm that an attempt to kidnap Monsieur Said Ben Hassi from his apartment in Avenue Georges Mandel at eight o'clock this evening resulted in a gun battle that claimed the lives of three people. These included the Minister's personal and private secretary Alphonse Belan and two as yet unidentified assailants. Speculation that this was in some way connected with the D'Orlac trial is premature. However, circumstantial evidence at the scene is indicative of that terror group's *modus operandus* and there is a logic to such an attempt on the premise that an exchange of prisoners could be forced upon the justice department.

*

Two days later . . .

The public bus was going down Rue Gambetta, heading for the outskirts. The weather had been gloomy during the first few weeks of October, then,

suddenly, an ochre sun burst signalled an unher-
alded 'Indian autumn'. The air was temporarily
mild, the sparse trees gold tinged and russet rinsed.
Sabine's old friend André Morel who had given the
Europol troopers the slip during the altercation in
Montparnasse and driven her to the 'hit' on Ackmann was standing on the open platform at the
back of the bus with a green canvas bag stretched
over his shoulder. A little way on he moved to a seat
halfway up the vehicle. For a while André sat admir-
ing the shapely neck of the woman sitting in front of
him, watching the golden hairs dance on her nape in
the gentle breeze coming in through the open window.

Down past the Place, along the Rue Belgrand,
André waited until the girl with the beautiful neck
got off, then reached into his bag twisted a switch
and pushed its bulky contents under the seat in
front of him. At square Edouard Vaillant he alighted
and caught a cab back to the Bois de Bologne. Later
on the radio he heard the explosion had killed ten
and injured thirty-six as the bus stopped in
Yvelinnes.

*

Summoning Fouvier to the ministry, Ben Hassi
hammered the table in front of him.

'These assassinations must end!' He was surrounded by Salafi Emirs from the proposed new
Umayyad caliphates of Abdul Rahman Al Ghafiqi,
Tariq ibn-Ziyad, and Umar asu Bakr, areas that
were formerly known as Aix-en-Provence, Vienne,
and Limousin. 'Make an example of this D'Orlac
woman,' they all insisted in unison, waggling their
fists and shaking their heads, '*Insha'Allah!*'

'Sir, we have succeeded in obtaining the whereabouts of one of the ringleaders of the subversive movement, Arnaud Bellew.'

'Then seize him!'

'Well, that may be difficult, he's actually in Germany giving lectures to the Bavarian underground.'

'Tell our friends in Munich. Arrange for The Brothers to do it and smuggle this *kuffar* bastard back over the border.'

'We must be careful not to offend the German Security Services.'

'Do not worry. They will not interfere. They will cooperate in the name of maintaining good community relations. We can have half a million of our people out on their streets within hours. Bonn knows this and will overlook this minor indiscretion on our part.'

Fouvier nodded obligingly. 'I will arrange it, Minister!'

Then by way of celebrating Ben Hassi's narrow escape from death, he and the Emirs booked a whole floor at a five star hotel and had a makeshift sheesheh bar set up in the corridor. Standing on the balcony overlooking the Tuileres they selected young girls walking below to be brought up to them. That afternoon, Said was in a particularly excitable state. He signalled for his Chaghoo-Kesh knife-puller men to stop a pretty blonde in a red skirt riding a bicycle. She kicked and struggled at first, but then he sliced off her nose with the curved blade of his *koummya*. When she fainted, he was free to ravish her in whatever way he liked.

'I like the fair skin of these *Parisiennes*, he said to his accomplices, 'it would be a sin to have to kill them all and destroy their city.'

*

In the middle of the afternoon, as Arnaud Bellew walked towards a private apartment in the swinging Schwabing district of Munich, he was accosted by two Chechens who spoke little French or German. At first he was taken aback, receiving heavy blows to his ribs and the side of his head, knocking his glasses into the road before going down under steel toe-capped kicks.

He felt them lift him by the arms, his feet dragging on the sidewalk as they moved his broken body towards the open door of a waiting car. Then, still not fully conscious, Bellew sensed a further commotion as a group of German students led by Dieter Vogel and Gabi Lange, who had been asked to look after him, stormed in like a leather-clad thunder clap, raining down karate chops on the would-be abductors, cracking noses and dislocating jaws in a rapid onslaught filled with curses and knuckle-dusters.

Two hours later, a telephone rang in the Brigade Criminelle on the Quai des Orfevres.

'If you want Bozh and Zhyogal back alive then release Sabine D'Orlac immediately,' came a whisper down the line.

The resistants' anticipated a negative response but they were determined to take advantage of the situation by implying that they would compromise the Eurabist front in the French government by exposing their ordering of secret service interference in another EU state.

Dieter and Gabi took footage of the Chechens, eyes covered and faces beetroot red after the abduction attempt. Arnaud spoke on the poorly recorded soundtrack.

'For everyone you kill, we will reply two-fold. But we are magnanimous: return *La Pétroleuse* and we'll spare these men. If you do not, we'll grant them the martyrdom they desire.'

Forty-eight hours later, no response had been forthcoming. Sometime in the early hours of the next morning, Bellew, who had been spirited back into France with Bodine's help, ordered the captives' swansong. YouTube carried a thirty second clip of German gun barrels being placed against the back of their heads and triggers being pulled, dead bodies slumping like grain sacks to the floor.

'We will match fire with fire!' was Bellew's parting shot.

*

Parking in and around the Île de la Cité was prohibited. The police were checking the passes of all the people milling about Rue de Harlay. Security measures were intense. They stopped the Volkswagen in Boulevard de Sebastopol and stepped out of the side doors, slipping into the shadows at the Rue Adolphe Adam. Luc had a Glok 19 tucked inside his bulky leather jacket. Franck Bodine had a Benelli Super 90 shotgun hidden inside a plastic mackintosh. Moving swiftly along the sidewalk, flinty jaws chipped and set for action, heading for La Conciergerie, they observed resistance commandos dressed as engineers pretending to work on some underground cabling at the side of the road and a familiar black Mercedes car occupied by an even more familiar couple embracing fervently further down the street.

Locked and loaded Dubois and Bodine passed through a police cordon, waving false ID papers they had been provided with by friends inside the system, giving them permission to access the area to the side of the court buildings. It began to spit rain as the big wooden door at the back entrance to the judiciary swung open, two armed officers and a female guard stepping through. Their captive recognised her liberators straightaway and smiled - deliriously as they pulled out their weapons and opened up from all quarters, taking the complacent security by complete surprise in a deadly cross fire.

The bullets were still flying, bodies falling as a smoke grenade was rolled into the road, its detonation filling the side street in smothering grey. Bodine used cutters to splice Sabine free from the chained corpses. Luc ushered her into the parked car where the erstwhile lovers, André Morel and Dominique Pascale were returning fire from shattered side windows. Luc reversed the car, ramming an oncoming police Nationale motorcyclist to the ground and broad-siding a Renault Scenic before racing off, leaving confusion and death in their wake.

On the Run

The city was bathed in a cold, loveless light. There was a drone of a motor in Luc's ears. All around the long rows of towering apartment blocks and gigantic glass-fronted commercial premises with glaring fluorescent lights flashed past the windows. The Mercedes was pretty shot up, barely fit for the job. The atmosphere was tense as they evaluated their circumstances.

'We need to get to Place De L'Alma before they block the embankment,' Luc said. Already, he could see Bellew's van lights in the rear view.

'Straight on, you can't miss it!' Sabine shouted.

'They're behind us, just two minutes and I'll pull over. Did anyone see what happened to Franck?'

'He got clear!' Sabine confirmed.

'How is André?' Luc called over his shoulder.

'Bad,' Dominique was sobbing. André's head was in her lap. His eyes were closed. Luc looked at Sabine. She frowned and shook her head. 'He's not breathing,' Dominique kept saying.

'Press down on his chest three times, then count to five and repeat!' Luc commanded.

Dominique, almost hysterical, slid out from under André's dangling limbs and mounted him on the back seat. Luc could see her working his rib cage in the mirror.

'Is he conscious?' Sabine called.

'*Non*, Just more blood,' Dominique cried.

In Place d'Iena, Luc brought the car to a halt. The white van that had tracked them from the Fountaine des Mers juddered to a stop and Arnaud Bellew oversaw the transfer as pre-planned, Sabine dragging Dominique by her red hair from André's oozing body. She was kicking and screaming until Luc slapped her hard across the face.

'We must go!'

Bellew's people slammed the door shut on them and they thundered off. In the back of the van Sabine lit cigarettes for everyone and they checked their ammo. Luc noticed Dominique had taken a shell. She winced when he insisted on treating it and began to bandage her abdomen. Dominique's face went pale and she passed out from loss of blood. The radio was on full blast. The news bulletin was dominated by their escape and simultaneous resistance machinegun attacks on the Europol sentry boxes under the arcades on the rue de Rivoli and the car bomb set off in front of the Palais du Luxembourg. The commentators criticised the authorities for their failure to deal with the insurgency and keep *La Pétroleuse* off the streets. Journalists harangued the Police Commissioners to explain how they were sealing off parts of the city in an attempt to isolate the criminals from areas of potential support.

'Too late,' Luc breathed, 'those fuckers don't control everywhere yet!'

A Kawasaki whizzed by them in an attempt to guide the van to its destination. In a small back street off Rue Descamps a safe house was opened up and they staggered inside with Dominique strung between them, eventually falling into bed, exhausted. Luc lay for hours listening to Sabine snoring loudly next to him, watching the musty wings of multi-coloured moths beat drum solos on the electric bulb hanging over them, before he too, gun in hand, fell into darkness.

*

Fouvier hustled into the back of Lieutenant Bruyere's car as soon as the message came over the radio.

'What's been happening?' The blood drained from his face. 'Amateurs!'

His fist crashed down on the dashboard. His driver threw a U-turn and gunned the car back along the Quai de Grenelle. Fouvier's ear was pinned to the mobile unit. The *Inspecteur* was picking up intermittent snatches of the story.

'Gun fight ... five dead ... D'Orlac spirited off ...' he robotically repeated.

A finger hit the radio switch.

'We'll have to maintain radio silence for this,' he said to Bruyere as the car shot through a red light in the onrushing Parisian twilight, 'It is clear they have infiltrators everywhere!'

In the distance the Eiffel Tower loomed catatonic on a dark horizon. The Black flag of the Prophet fluttered from its apex, defiant in the light of the city burning below.

'They will try to get her out of Paris as soon as possible. We must seal off the airports and railway stations with immediate effect. Get all available men out onto the streets in a show of strength, set up road blocks at all key junctions.' Then, almost shamefacedly, 'Offer money to any informers we have amongst them,' tapping the side of his head, 'and get Costello on the line to me as soon as you can.'

He hated asking for the Englishman's help but he had no choice. Politicos like Ben Hassi would be calling for his head. The powerful Equality Commission would throw the book at him.

*

EXECUTIVE ORDER 7738531/SBH

In the city itself, I authorise the most energetic counter-revolutionary actions. Martial law is now in force. Destroy any districts that offer any form of resistance. Hang all rebel organisers upon capture. Evacuate any home, street, or quarter where we believe *La Pétroleuse* may take shelter and burn them down. D'Orlac must be taken alive, Dubois and the others shot on sight. Prepare the explosive devices on the bridges across the Seine, then, if the Right Bank falls, we will hold the Left.

ISSUED FROM
THE OFFICE OF SAID BEN HASSI

*

Large parts of the city burst into flame that night. Incendiaries were everywhere. While Bodine marshalled his campaign, fighting hand to hand in the streets, Bellew had returned to the strongpoint in Belleville to issue broadcasts across the airwaves.

Government troops supported by Fellagha fanatics were brutally crushing any pockets of opposition they came across. Summary executions were commonplace. Torpid bodies of men and women swung before the cracking glass in burnt out buildings around the Île de la Cité. Over three hundred were killed before the bells struck midnight. Bodine himself had narrowly escaped capture in an attack on the new mosque on rue de Bruxelles, shooting his way out while some of his most loyal commandos ran suicide missions all around him. From the attic of a third floor apartment in the city's Eighteenth *Arrondissement*, Alun Thomas peered down over the rooftops, staring through the sombre blackout, his eyes barely able to see the stumbling figures running around in the afterglow of the firestorm below. Like so many others, this militant from Meibion Glyndwr, who had been seconded from his farm in Powys to act as European Liaison Officer, lifted a MK II's scope to his face, his red dragon shoulder badge rubbing against his ear. He was mindful of the importance attached to every bullet he could let off before he was taken. Within a few minutes three robed Mohammedans were lying dead, holes through the centre of their heads, staining the flagged surface of the Place du Tertre with their foreign blood.

'Words are not enough anymore,' he whispered to himself as the gun butt kicked against his shoulder. 'Bullets are my new metaphors!'

Arnaud Bellew knew Paris was the hinge upon which the destiny of his country swung. He could see in his mind's eye Sainte-Chapelle, the Sacre Cœur and the Arc de Triomphe, three sublime and resonant monuments, staring back in bewilderment at what was befalling the *city of light*. Arnaud felt this place was the fulcrum, all the major road and

rail links intersected here. It was where the treas-
ures of Empires were set out on display and some of
the greatest advances of science, art, sculpture, and
medicine were celebrated. For his opponents, like
Said Ben Hassi, however, it represented something
else: an imperialism and triumphalism that evi-
denced their own people's millennia of inadequacy
and that had become an object for their spleen, no
more than a stage for their theatrical revenge.

Bellew felt that the first salvo in a new war for
European survival was being fired. How would
France's neighbours respond? Would the Scots of
William Wallace; the Irish of Fion mac Cumhaill;
the Welsh of Owain; the English of Henry; the
Dutch of De Ruyter; the Belgians of Degrelle; the
Swedes of Ingvar the Far-Travelled; the Norwegians
of Harald Hardrada; the Finns of Lauri Allan Torni;
the Danes of Holger Danske; the Austrians of Peter
Mayr; and the Germans of Arminius from the
Teutoburger Wald rush to fill the gap in the battle
lines, to secure Europe, to defend Western civilisation? He held his breath and clutched the Celtic
cross banner hanging from the wall beside him.

*

In the Paris Headquarters of the Civil Defence
Authority, Ben Hassi was being briefed by the heads
of his security forces in a blacked out conference
room. He listened intently above the whirr of
ventilation equipment, the chirrup of plasma
screens and the constant interruption of telephone,
sms and email updates coming in from the troops
and informers with boots on the ground.

Claude Levangie was sitting to the left of the
Minister. Ben Hassi studiously ignored him while
everyone else spoke. Then, when the Head of State

Security tried to open his mouth the bitter Mohammedan clicked his fingers and two of his robed assistants stepped forward to drag Levangie away from the table. All witnessed his summary execution by knife before the Minister pointed out the simple fact:

'From now on failure will not be tolerated!'

'Minister,' General Fabius Leclerc continued nervously, 'we have assumed control of all key areas.' Then, pointing to a large three dimensional electronic display screen showing Paris, sector by sector, he began to outline his plans for containment and stop and search. Ben Hassi pondered for a moment.

'And where are the African contingents?'

Leclerc indicated with a pointer device. 'Here, here, and here,'

'Losses?'

'Thirty police, fifty two Europol Militia, twelve army and sixteen from our African Partner states.'

'That is acceptable,' the Minister confirmed.

'We have taken six or seven of their people alive, including some foreign nationals. Most fight to the death or commit suicide.'

'Any leads?'

'Not yet. But to be honest our specialists have not got to them.'

'They must be made to talk. Hand them over to the *mujahidin* if they do not break quickly. Time is of the essence.'

'Certainly Minister.'

Ben Hassi lifted a black marker pen and walked over to the flat screen on the wall, drawing a big cross on the surface for dramatic effect.

'Gentlemen,' he said 'you have seen my executive order. Paris must be cleansed. These guerrillas are an affront to God. The streets must be purified, regardless of the damage or destruction this may cause. Bring whatever forces you have to bear on this issue.'

*

The next morning, Luc and Sabine woke up early. The air was cool but dry. Already people had come out picking up dead relatives along the quais by the Seine or fishing bodies out of the muddy waters. At the safe house the shutters were drawn. Dust lay everywhere like dandruff. Luc followed Sabine into the dining room. Seventies' wallpaper hung down in strips. There was a smell of something stagnant lying hidden behind the sofa in the sitting room where an old piano stood forlorn under a diamante-style light. Sabine threw open a kitchen cupboard and the clattering sound sent a black furry shape scurrying into the hallway, cat's claws scratching on bare floorboards. Luc leaned back in a soft armchair bracing himself for what might come next.

'A lot of people must have died last night,' he said.

'It wasn't a genuine insurrection, was it?'

'It was cover for your escape.'

Sabine watched him for a moment, trying to put out of her mind the scale of the sacrifice. Then she grabbed his hand and pulled his unwilling arm after her as she moved back towards the wide-open staircase.

'We've got the place to ourselves!' she shouted, moving like a whirlwind up the steps and through the empty bedrooms. Flinging the doors open to the radiant winter light, she was laughing, screaming, 'I'm free! I'm free!'

He was caught up in her joy.

'You have no idea,' she said 'what it is like being kept in solitary for weeks on end.'

With her chin thrust upwards, she advanced on him, big brown eyes flashing vividly.

'You know what I want,' she mocked.

Luc could smell the sugar-sweet tang of sexual excitement running from her pores. He followed her from room to room. In a slope-roofed attic they came across a flowered pitcher on a washstand and a tattered mattress thrown carelessly onto a metal bed frame. It immediately brought back memories of their first place together.

They sat down. Sabine raised one knee, holding it with both hands. 'Now, about that semen . . . '

'You can't be serious' Luc said.

'I've been living like a nun,' she insisted, before standing and jumping up, using the bed like a tired trampoline, 'Who do you think I am, Joan of Arc?'

'Some people think you are!'

Sabine giggled, 'I am no virgin!'

Her head was nearly touching the highest beam before she lost balance, tipping sideways in a wild flurry of arms and tumbling black locks, hitting the floor hard. Luc grabbed her head. The cheeks were white and cold. He thought she was unconscious. He could feel a pulse as he bent down to give the kiss of life but she opened her eyes, her mouth a gurgling drain of merry-making.

'You see,' she was stuttering, 'I knew you wanted me!'

'I was worried,' he protested.

Sabine rolled over, clambering to her feet, when suddenly her expression changed completely into an ink black smudge of grief. Dominique was there in the doorway, half dressed, looking utterly disgusted. 'Please, don't stop, on my account,' she insisted.

Sabine pushed by Luc and took Dominique by the arm.

'*Comment ça-va?*' she asked.

'André's dead!' she kept repeating as Sabine led her back down the long staircase.

Luc watched them go as he slumped over the top banister. Dominique walked with her head tilted towards Sabine. She was completely defeated. The bandages around her belly coming loose.

'*À quoi bon?*' she kept asking between dry chesty gasps.

'*C'est à n'y pas croire!*'

Luc eventually followed them into the sparse sitting room. Sabine had laid Dominique out on the sofa and draped a woollen blanket over the wreckage of the former government agent.

'Play something,' Sabine begged, gesturing towards the upright piano. Luc walked over and lifted its varnished lid. Sabine lit him a Camel and pushed over an ashtray. He sat down and opened the score, starting tentatively to tinkle out Liszt's piano sonata in B minor. The ease with which his fingers flowed over the vaguely tuned keyboard surprised him. He blew smoke rings up towards the ghastly imitation crystal chandelier and watched the girls watching him.

Eventually Dominique was talked into taking another sedative and she slipped off into sleep. Sabine came over, leaning on the side of the piano, holding her head in her hands. Luc saw her swirling a teardrop as it fell onto the dark wood, her small fingertips tracing wet silver on the piano's surface.

'André died to save me!' He nodded. 'Why did it come to this?'

'Because he, like all the others, believed!'

'Believed?'

'In you, *La Pétroleuse!*'

Sabine waved a hand, 'That is ridiculous!'

'No, it is not. Do you have any idea what an icon you have become?'

*

Luc's car stopped outside the supermarket to pick up some groceries and a bottle of red.

'We're going to get out of the city, pretty soon,' he told his driver, 'They are combing the suburbs for her.'

'Bellew's got everything planned,' the man said, 'I'll be your guide, don't worry, we won't let you down.'

Luc patted him on the shoulder, got out and skipped up the steps through sliding doors. He had a wad of money from well-wishers. Inside, wanted posters for members of the resistance were prominently displayed in the grey concrete entrance hall. He noted a particularly unflattering photograph of himself and smirked before collecting what he needed, paying cash and winking at the cashier. Returning with a plastic bag full of fresh food he insisted they went back via a pharmacy so that he could buy surgical pads and clean bandages to sterilise Dominique's wound.

'How is she?' the driver asked from behind the wheel.

'The doctor got the bullet out,' Luc said, 'but somehow the wound got infected. He's given her antibiotics but she stays in bed most of the time and screams a lot in her sleep.'

'You know, the news report said they had returned André's body to his family . . . '

'Yeah.'

'Well, don't tell Dominique, but it is a lie: the Harkis strung it up in an interrogation cell and showed it to detainees to frighten them.'

'Fuck!'

'They are absolute bastards. One day we'll repay them!'

*

Two days later, at a little after seven thirty in the evening, as part of a major surge through the city the Europol arrived at an apartment in Joinville le-Pointe. Inside, an Englishman whose passport identified him as Steve Smith, and who purported to be a trainee architect, stashed his Spanish pistol in his back pocket, opening the door with a smile.

'Bonjour,' he said helpfully, but when the police attempted forced entry he pulled the Astra 300 and killed two before being hauled to the ground and heavily beaten. Twelve hours later, after a summary hearing on charges of being a gun runner for the resistance, Smith, whose real name was Kevin Edge, found himself standing before a garrotte in a small cell, under the main police headquarters in Issy-les-Moulineaux.

'You'll never beat us,' he cursed as dark hands manoeuvred his face towards the wooden mecha-nism. 'Like a great man once said when the English fight we will throw everything at you including the kitchen sink!'

At the same time a police report was being filed in Bougivol. Gendarmes had by all accounts stopped a silver blue BMW on the A13 and a female driver and a male accomplice, answering the descriptions of two known criminal aliens from Western Ger-many, Dieter Vogel and Gabi Lange, had driven off at high speed. Having apparently given chase, the

BMW hit a wall outside Vaucresson and the occupants got out, offering up intermittent small arms fire as the police and militia surrounded them. The available information indicated that Vogel was killed by a bullet to the chest. It was confirmed that Gabi had apparently decided to surrender, walking out into the open with a jacket over her arm. When requested to drop her coat Miss Lange refused to comply and she was shot with a single round to the head. Upon examining the corpse the gendarmerie reported they had found an explosive device in the folds of the Afghan jacket. It seemed Bellew's question was being answered. Committed activists from across the continent were beginning to infiltrate France through the channels and networks set up by the resistance. The Battle for Europe had commenced.

*

Ben Hassi arrived at the tented city in front of the Institut de France around nine in the evening. Walking through the maze of impossibly narrow alleys in St-Germain-des-Pres surrounded by a troop of his Revolutionary Guards, he was ready to mourn the martyrs who had fought and died to capture the city. A makeshift mosque was already filled to capacity with men dressed in black shirts; women in black chadors and young girls in headscarves. As he entered Said was greeted by a delegation of Sunni, Shia, and Wahabi mullahs, fresh from their *ghalyoun* pipes. He made the sign of Arabic brotherhood and went forward, a path clearing before him in a great U shape that swept all around the mosque.

While they waited for the ceremony to begin, he was offered a small glass of tea and took the opportunity to toast the ancient martyr Iman Hossein. 'Will there be the traditional *zanjeer-zani*?' he enquired, with a sweet, hot breath.

'We have ordered the chains, your excellency,' a courtier in robes bowed. With a wave of his finger Said signalled his impatience for the formalities to begin. An imam moved to a microphone stand and began the ritual chant. Then a column of men, sometimes even very young boys marched forward across the Pont des Arts, each headed by a standard bearer; each raising a clenched hand in the air and then bringing it down hard, beating their chests in time with the rhythmic call of the master of ceremonies.

The women looked on as some young fanatics took the *ghammeh*, running the tips of their blades across dusky foreheads, blood pouring onto the floor.

'Look at the dedication of our young people,' Ben Hassi said, as an aside to the *mullahs* congregated about him, 'Where are the sons of Bonaparte now?'

*

'Dim the lights a minute,' Luc said as he walked over to one of the tall windows, glanced down through a gap in the curtains, and instantly stiffened. Sabine saw his reaction and froze.

'What is it?' She was by his shoulder in an instant.

'They are standing down there in the shop doorway.'

'I can see them. What are they doing?'

'The way they look . . . they look hard,' he pondered out loud.

'Police?' Sabine was staring down into the street.

'No one would be out there unless they had to be?'

'A couple of our friends?'

'It's possible. But why weren't we told?'

Further down the road they could see the watchers' car parked up on the kerb. A tall and a short man stood staring up at the the house. The shorter of the two wore a trilby hat and was rubbing his hands.

'Is there enough petrol in our car?'

He nodded, walked over to the coat rack, threw on a dark overcoat, and pulled a woollen hat over his fair hair.

'Get me a knife, a big one!'

Sabine went through to the kitchen and came back brandishing a bread carver. Luc slipped it up his sleeve.

'Bolt the back door behind me,' he said.

She led him down to the rear entrance. As he went out the cold rush of early evening wind pecked at his flesh like a bird. He could see his own breath.

Luc walked slowly along the sidewalk, a shadow on grey, fissured cement. He could see the two men clearly. A car came up the street and he stepped out of its beams, down a side alley. The vehicle drifted by. While his adversaries' eyes were blinded by the passing headlights, Luc peered around the corner. They had not moved. He watched them lighting cigarettes and shifting from foot to foot in a futile attempt to stay warm.

Moving further off down the alley he circled the block, moving around behind them, coming up by their car. He lurched into the road on all fours, crawling over frosty cobblestones until he was within arms' reach of the rear off-side wheel. The knife went in first time. The gentle hiss of escaping air was barely audible in the empty darkness. He repeated the process, stabbing the other rear tyre. Then, retracing his footsteps, came back under Sabine's cover as she stood by the window, wooden frame slightly ajar, a Russian Bizon machine pistol hanging off her shoulder.

'What do you think?' she asked, as she eased off the bolt and he stepped back inside the house.

'Security service,' Luc breathed, 'Got to be!'

'Why don't they come for us then?'

'Maybe they are just suspicious or are trying to entrap others.'

'Maybe they think we have hostages.'

'Possibly.'

They went back to the upstairs window and watched as the taller man stepped out of the shadows to toss a cigarette butt in the gutter.

'Just two?'

'Looks like it.'

'We have a choice,' Sabine whispered, 'leave now or stay and risk a siege.'

'What about Dominique? She's not fit to travel?'

'She's not coming!'

'But if we leave her they'll interrogate . . .' Luc broke off as Sabine made a clear and final gesture regarding the problem.

'But . . . '

'She knew the rules when she joined. We're not leaving anyone or carrying excess baggage.'

As Luc packed some clothes and small arms into duffel bags, Sabine buttoned her long blue coat, selected a cushion, and walked up the staircase towards the room where Dominique slept.

A few minutes later, she returned wiping her eyes and speaking in broken monosyllables. 'We walk out as if we are going for a drink, OK. No rush, no panic. You open the car doors and we get in. I use the gun only if they shoot.'

'Understood!'

They opened the front door and loaded the car. The two men in the doorway stepped out into the road. Luc and Sabine exchanged a knowing look and Luc hammered down on the accelerator, pulling away from their opponents, who, having run back to their car, and realised what had happened, pulled out mobile phones, calling Bruyere's men for back up.

*

'Christ!' Costello moaned from his bed in Wimbledon. 'You are sure it was them?'

'Sure, boss. We saw them clearly as they drove by. We've contacted Fouvier's people and Bruyere's got an alarm out.' There was personal concern in his voice. He knew that *La Pétroleuse* always fulfilled her threats and that he was a key target.

'They'll be in deep with their supporters again by now.'

'I know. They'll probably have changed cars and IDs already. These people are better than our Irish adversaries. More united.'

'They have their backs up against the wall. It is a nightmare over there.'

'Tell me about it. We are never sure who is in charge—the French or the Arabs?'

'Don't ask difficult questions!' Costello warned. 'Just stick to Fouvier and try to avoid Ben Hassi's mercenaries. Ok? They are too excited about their own agendas. Our job is simple: work with the French Security Service until told otherwise.'

The Special air services operative was already thinking about sending his wife and children away for safety. He did not want them caught up in this vendetta.

'At some point someone is going to have to ask questions, though. Some of the things we are witnessing are beyond the pale.'

'Black Ops are Black Ops. You know what we have done in Iraq and what we did in the former Yugoslavia. We get the job done.'

'Boss, I know, but I wouldn't want this stuff going on in Berkshire.'

'That's why we are doing it in France!' Costello said, hoping that the conversation would end there; the thought of his own government's cowardice in the face of the political and religious demands of the exploding ethnic population in Great Britain set his teeth on edge. Organised movements were already forming across the UK, replicating the resistance across the channel.

*

A mid afternoon breeze ran a cold wet tongue over the windscreen. Luc's eyes were fixed on the road. Every time he saw a gendarme he began to recite the Lord's prayer, despite the special security pass on the windshield, giving them *carte blanche* to leave the city.

'Must not go over the limit,' he kept telling himself.

His foot moved stiffly on the accelerator. It seemed almost unwilling to release the pressure. Pulling up outside a school, a column of kindergarten children passed in front of his radiator grill. A woman with a large bag of laundry pressed against his passenger door, trying to squeeze between the cars.

'God damn,' he said to himself, 'This is like being in a goldfish bowl.'

The car slipped silently over the Pont Neuf, where limp white bodies hung on hooks from street lights. Below, the Seine ran a vivid brown diarrhoea to the left and right as far as the eye could see. Public executions by Europol militia were daily events now as the mask of civilisation slipped even further and revenge attacks by Berber patrols on real or imagined anti-Eurabic dissidents went unpunished. Luc could see bodies lying unattended on the street. Down the Rue Daphine and across the busy junction of Saint-Germain he noticed the big green expanse of the Jardin du Luxembourg had become a tented city. The Renault was like a salmon swimming upstream against a tide of people moving towards roadside bazaars that had sprung up to service and profiteer from the newcomers. Luc felt a sickly chill in the pit of his stomach.

'Must keep going,' he told himself.

Swirling the Place d'Italie, they span off into the outer districts.

'Don't forget you take the next junction for Bretigny Sur-Orge,' he remembered Sabine had said, pointing at the map with her finger.

He flicked a button and the heater came on, the engine ticking over warm and easy as it moved into more open country. Columns of military trucks passed them by. Trees raised their bare knotty arms in prayer against the yellow-grey skyline. Luc followed a looping river for a kilometre or two before heading for Étampes, stopping as instructed on an embankment of churned dirt. The mushy yellow grass was soft and greasy underfoot. He moved around to the back of the car and opened the boot. Sabine's smile greeted him as the metal lifted slowly on a lazy hinge.

'Told you,' she said reassuringly, stepping out onto the riverbank before they both pressed their shoulders against the back of the car to push. Once it was rolling it could not be stopped. The Renault plunged into the sucking brown water, sinking right up to its windows in seconds, and then, turning slightly with the current, dipping below the waves as their muddy contours interlaced over the roof, it disappeared out of sight.

'What now?' he asked Sabine.

'We wait!'

*

From the road the country on either side looked dead. Endless woods spread over the expanse of flatland and very occasionally a small stream would cut its way through a valley in a swirling torrent of icy razor blades. Houses and villages seemed to cling to the earth here, despite the endless grey sky that came rushing down like Noah's flood to wash them away over each sloping horizon.

The car wheels kept turning, grazing the wet N60 as the windscreen wipers moved over the glass. Orleans was clogged in the threadbare skeins of the misty Loire—or the Owar, as it was signposted in Arabic, the avenues and streets leading off in all directions, radiating like the twisting tentacles of a stretching stone octopus. Old blocks, some four or five stories tall, built of granite and covered in green mould, stood proud to the sky, the stains of the passing years dribbling down the brickwork. Metal shutters sprayed with graffiti hung at angles from upper floors. They crossed the river on a ramshackle of rutted stanchions. Below them, the smoky grey water seemed fast and furious. A fine drizzle blew in from the east. They could see thin, bleak figures foraging around the market place.

Sabine sat next to him, reading from a book, 'Ancient Genabum, conquered by Caesar in 52 BC and renamed Aurelianus, besieged by Attila's hordes, and eventually taken by Clovis in AD 498.'

'It's where the Saviour Maid stood against the English,' Luc remembered.

The car was circling around the Ste-Croix Cathedral. The façade was covered in an intricate lattice of stonework, forming twin towers that spiralled upwards into the low cloud formations. Following Sabine's directions, they cut a diagonal across the heart of the city, pulling into the side of the road once they recognised their location. Luc, with a swift jerk, applied the hand-break. Ice-cold water tip-tapped on the thin tin hood as he got out and went up to the door, knocking gently.

Ten minutes later he was back, keys hanging from his fingers. Sabine smiled nervously.

'Everything OK?' she asked.

'We've got an apartment nearby in the Rue de Carmes.'

Fighting with an umbrella against the wind, they unloaded their gear and Luc drove off to exchange cars with some friends of the movement.

*

Fouvier walked into Ben Hassi's office with a leather briefcase swinging at his side. The Interior Justice Minister was almost shaking with indignation.

'Fouvier, tell me when these bandits will be captured?' he bellowed. 'I am seriously asking myself if our French allies should lead on this issue.'

'In the interests of presenting a united front, Minister, I think it would be tactically disastrous to take any other route. This way at least a portion of the indigenous French will hesitate to take up arms.'

'Yes, the advantages of collaborating has got us so far but President Belaire's time is running out. The benefits of divide and rule are decreasing. Our forces now represent the civic authority across whole sections of this country and we are imposing the *shari'ah* by decree. I want these resisters to feel their subjugation to Allah's godly and righteous judgement, sooner rather than later.'

'Minister, we are capturing and taking out many of their operative units on a daily basis. Admittedly the D'Orlac trial backfired but she is in hiding, not fighting! Costello will be back in France soon and will run her to ground. With both Dubois and *La Pétroleuse* out of the picture the likes of Bodine, Bellew, and the rest will face a severe haemorrhage of talent.'

'The Coalition of Government and Eurabian armed forces lost over four hundred men last week!'

'I know.' Fouvier acknowledged.

'These infidels are fighting back and getting in-creasing amounts of foreign support. I want more severe reprisals. Double the reward on D'Orlac's head and make it clear we will flatten any city, town, or village that shelters her and this Dubois charac-ter.'

'I will,' Fouvier said, responding to the waved dismissal from behind Ben Hassi's desk. He turned to exit the office.

'And Fouvier,' The minister added threateningly, 'Please act swiftly. In fact, act as if your life de-pended on it!'

The *Inspecteur*'s car returned along the Quai des Orfevres. Ten minutes later, Fouvier was back at his bureau overlooking Grand Augustins on the Left Bank, pondering his options. Anticipating problems, he, like Costello, had already sent his wife Amélie to stay with relatives in London. His only daughter was working for the UN in New York. A knock on the door interrupted his thoughts.

'Come in.' It was Bruyere, with a print out of an e-report from a small surveillance centre in the Indre.

'We have a potential sighting,' Bruyere spluttered excitedly, 'some photos and an address!'

'Where?'

'Orléans!'

'Can we be sure?'

'We've had these digital images relayed, look for yourself.'

Fouvier took a moment to take in what was before him. 'That's Dubois and D'Orlac,' he concluded, 'Where is our friend Mr Costello now?'

'Just got to Saint-Malo.'

*

They had been in the city two weeks, driving out in the winter rain to see the sleet encrusted chateaux at Chambord, Blois, and Amboise. At night they went to the Dirty Pea, slipping in the back door to eat *paté de lapereau*. Back in the apartment hard rain slapped the window.

'Spiders!' she would screech, 'Spiders! Big black and ugly . . .' Luc turned on the light. She was bolt upright, tight as a drum skin. Her arms outstretched. 'There,' she said, 'Can you see them?' Luc looked into her expressionless face.

'There's nothing there,' he assured her.

'They were coming, I tell you. Hundreds of them crawling towards me.'

'You were dreaming.'

He wrapped his arms around her, but she shrugged him off, drawing her knees up to her chin.

'I don't want them near me, do you hear!'

Unable to sleep, Sabine stood watching the rivulets running down the roadside, carrying sludgelike dog excrement towards the drains. The sewers overfilled and the drainpipes rattled. The slates on the apartment moved sometimes in the wind keeping them both awake. Pacing was her thing. She could not bear just waiting for things to happen. In the early hours of the morning she would stand for ages watching the drunks catcall each other and the street girls plying their trade. Occasionally, a police car would cruise by scattering the kerb crawlers. She would follow the lights as they flicked from red and green through the falling sheets of rain.

Waking up late they would eat cereals and drink freshly squeezed juice. Sabine was studying Evola's *Yoga of Power* and undertaking tantric exercises to keep limber. After lunch they went out and walked across the street to an incommunicado meeting with Franck Bodine. A heavy mist hung over the city like a Biblical curse. Even the birds were mute in the trees. Luc bought a newspaper from an old man who was stamping his feet on a cold slab corner. Sabine watched as the eczema-cracked skin on the vendor's fingers stirred the change in the front pocket of the cloth apron slung about his neck. Someone asked directions to the Musée Historique and the seller explained in great detail, keeping Luc waiting until he had finished.

'Merci,' Luc said, then turning to Sabine, 'There's the place; let's get something warm to eat.' Moving slowly along the pavement they checked out an alternate exit should they need it.

Inside, the ever-avuncular Bodine sat alone at the zinc. Another man, of indeterminate age, was propped at a corner table with a Browning automatic under a folded newspaper. Sabine threw her arms about Bodine's strong neck and kissed him on both cheeks.

'It is good to see you, uncle!' she screamed. Luc and Franck shook hands manfully. Bodine looked tired, soapy eye-sockets greeting them with a benevolent smirk.

'Everything OK?' they asked, ordering coffees.

'Good,' he nodded, slipping a brown envelope filled with money to Luc across the counter, 'This is your share of the inheritance from Aunt Dominique's estate. Your cousins all send their fondest regards.'

'Long journey?' Luc asked.

'I've been driving all night. I'm a little car sick that's all.' He took a large swig from the cup in his hand. 'What about you guys, enjoying your vacation?'

'Yes,' Sabine said, 'but I'll need to be back at work soon. I miss my job.'

'Yes, I know my partner Mr Bellew is keen to have you back.'

'Tell him, I'll be ready,' the girl said climbing off the stool she had taken, heading for the ladies to change her tampon. Bodine looked at Luc's face after her back was turned.

'She's eager?'

'Very!'

'You two OK?'

'Yes, just it isn't easy you know. We find it hard to sit on our hands.'

Bodine nodded in sympathy. 'I can imagine, she's a tigress.'

'So what's the latest. Do we just wait?'

' I think so. The decision in Paris was to give you the money and make sure you were mentally OK.'

'Mentally?'

'Well, you know, assess your psychological state?'

Bodine winked before buying them food and discussing future employment possibilities in euphemisms that amused all parties. Getting a signal from his team, Bodine kissed Sabine's hand and looked knowingly at Luc before evaporating with his Browning-wielding bodyguard into the car fumes outside.

Later, down by the riverside, they noticed the city smelled of oil and forgotten cargoes long gone to rot. Walking down Rue Royale, they followed the high black wall running down the Quai Cypierre. Luc's attention kept coming back and back again to the face of the figure walking at his side. He stopped to light a cigarette as she turned to look out over the expanse of the river. Her eyes were full of twisting currents like conga eels tangled in a net.

'I don't know how to ask you?' he began haltingly.

She began to pay him some vague attention, still staring out into the fathomless depths, mesmerized by the water.

'I love you,' Luc said, 'and I want to marry you!'

She hardly acknowledged his words. Sabine had given herself over to the rhythm of the waves lapping against the concrete. Luc was not sure she had even heard him. Sabine did not move or even blink. Finally she just whispered that was really silly given their circumstances. Luc felt foolish.

'I'm sorry,' he stumbled, attempting to brushover his *faux pas* with a banal apology. 'I don't know what I am thinking. Perhaps being on the run is getting to me.'

His denial however stung her from her trance. Sabine's eyes left the river and found his hurt face staring back at her.

'Don't you want to marry me?' she said, 'Never say that!'

She stepped towards him, reaching out for his arm. Her dark hair blew against his cheek as they made their way back along the embankment, looking out over the Pont George V, hand grenades in their pockets.

*

Costello took the call from Fouvier as he was checking into the hotel. A young blonde was tapping in his reservation details while a Negro carried suitcases towards a narrow staircase.

'Yes,' Costello agreed, 'we must take a chance. My team can't get there until morning. Are these people up to it?'

'I have no idea. Fouvier stumbled but it is our first positive ID and we can hope to take them by surprise.'

'They will fight!'

'Dead or alive, it is all the same to me.'

'Careful, you are beginning to sound like Ben Hassi.'

'I'm quoting him. It's them or me!' Costello's eyes narrowed.

'I see!'

'You do?'

'Yes, Sabine has promised to kill me and I think she intends to keep her word.'

'Then you have no choice, you must terminate her.'

'I know.'

*

A few minutes later, in a small bachelor's apartment in Dinan, a resistance supporter in the Service was pacing up and down, listening intently to what he was being told by Bruyere's secretary. The scene about him was chaotic: piles of books, torn newspaper cuttings, and journals were spread out over every available surface: settee, chairs, table, bed.

'They've located *La Pétroleuse*! I see. Mobilising local units. That must mean they do not want to wait to mount a big operation. Probably worried about leaks. They could have a squad there in no time now they've got the go ahead. *Merci* Sylvie. Leave it to me.'

The phone rang in the middle of the night and Luc answered it. A coded message was issued down the line.

What is it?' she asked.

'We've been compromised. We have to go.'

'How long have we got?'

'Now,' Luc said, slapping her feet, 'move!'

They ran about the place pulling together whatever they could in the semi-darkness. Ten minutes later they were in the car driving through blinding rain, big droplets bouncing like golf balls off the roof—jumping red lights, speeding away, leaving behind them the circling sound of militia alarms as they drove out beyond the city's outskirts, heading south towards Lyon.

*

John Costello flicked off the switch on his mobile and rose from the table, leaving his breakfast tray almost untouched. Walking over to the window he lit another Marlboro light and gazed at the bronze statue of the explorer Jacques Cartier beyond his balcony.

'Idiots,' he murmured almost imperceptibly.

Then, as the realisation of how close they had come to trapping her kicked in, a *sotto voce* tirade of epithets for the *Sûreté* leeched out into the air of his small hotel room.

The hard-copy files on Dubois and D'Orlac lay open on the bedside cabinet. Pin-point sightings and photos of them walking on the Quai Cypierre were on display. He could tell it was her at first glance. Those eyes once seen could never be forgotten. That almost imperceptible flick of the hair that was so endearing to vulnerable men. Just for a second, he felt a pang of jealousy against Dubois, but cast the foolishness aside, acknowledging the age difference between himself and his target.

'My job is to kill her not marry her,' he corrected himself. 'And now I have no option, because otherwise she will come for me!'

Dressing quickly, he packed his accoutrements, before paying his bill and setting out on the road for Orléans. Costello could usually hide his emotions beneath an affable professional façade, but on this occasion he was personally invested. The Special Air Services man was becoming increasingly concerned that it was himself or at least Fouvier's people that cornered these Bonnie and Clyde characters rather than the brigades of newly imported fanatics from north of the Sahara. Costello had witnessed some of their handiwork in a prison in Reims and did not particularly enjoy watching women's fingers being cut off one by one until they talked. For him, the boundaries between official and unofficial methods were becoming increasingly stark and dividing along religious and ethnic lines. What was happening in France appalled him and the moment this particular mission was over and his moral debt to Fouvier paid off he fully intended returning here to Saint-Malo, taking a ferry to Portsmouth, and never coming back over La Manche.

*

A census conducted on behalf of the Bureau of population studies reveals that the indigenous French are already a statistical minority in one third of southern Departments.

Budget forecasts released by the Social Care Institute identify a fifty percent increase in child care subsidies for immigrant communities within the last 18 months

The High Command in Paris withdraws the French navy from its Mediterranean bases after complaints that its presence is provocative to its developing world neighbours.

President Belaire indicates his intention to resign on state television. The stated reason is to spend more time with his new wife who was born in Haifa and to write a three-volume set of memoirs entitled *France et Moi*.

Autoroute
du Soleil

They had been driving for nearly two hours before they saw the outline of a bastide on the hilltop. Luc stopped at the sign that read *'Bienvenue dans le village de Domme.'*

Sabine lit her penultimate cigarette and nodded. 'We're hungry and we're broke!'

'I know.'

Their C5 crawled up the hill, its languid bends falling away into the rocky crevasse of the Dordogne river. They swept through the Porte des Bos, coming to a halt outside a small store. Luc slipped a Polish MAG-95 semi-automatic pistol inside his shirt, got out and swaggered over to the shop like a poor imitation of Jean Paul Belmondo in *Boute de Souffle*. Sabine stayed in the car, passenger door thrown wide open, her shoes firmly planted on the dusty road. She was melting red Lebanese over the hot lick of a lighter flame, crumbling it between her thumb and forefinger into some cigarette papers.

All was still and quiet. Smoke trails rose from chimneys on the ancient, bent, and twisted buildings. It was a traditional Batir, built during the Hundred Years War. There was a large arcaded market with a covered hall lying at the centre of a grid of streets running at right angles from the church square. The narrow alleys were divided by androne, a sort of mediaeval firebreak, so that if the town came under attack from either the English or the French crown it was less vulnerable to burning arrows.

Sabine folded the rizzlas and fired up her spliff, sucking hard on the mix of French tobacco and dope. She saw a man setting up a flower stand in the portico of the town hall and wished she could afford to buy a bunch of green-winged orchids. Children played with Barbie dolls on the external staircase of a house festooned with vines, potted geraniums, and begonias. Here in the southwest of the department, the river cut between two distinct regions, the Landais to the north and the Bergeracois to the south. The area was sparsely populated and she could see from the promontory the acres and acres of forests, battling brigades of native trees fighting off the advance of the maritime pine. She recalled learning in school about how peasants had grown plums, peaches, and maize here for centuries. She also remembered hearing recently from some comrades that in the Bergeracois village of Limeuil, a delightful old-walled citadel overlooking the confluence of the Dorgogne and the Vézère two fellow resistants from Rue Étienne Dolet had been cornered by the authorities and after a short hearing were tied to stakes and shot to death in a cold echo of the epuration of 1944-45. She shuddered and reached for the re-assurance of the carbine secreted inside the car, loosening the safety catch, eyes wide.

Meanwhile, the shopkeeper was out back loading some cartons into a delivery van when he heard Luc come in. He paid no attention at first, thinking it was one of his regular customers, but then caught sight of a young man's legs, stretching half off the ground, clearly reaching over the counter, his hands rattling at the till. The owner moved around to the cabin of his vehicle and slipped a hunting rifle out of a leather sheath. His fingers loaded the cartridges like he was shooting grouse. A bead of sweat ran down his forehead, but otherwise he moved confidently like an experienced *chasseur*.

The first shot tore through the wood-bench millimetres from Luc's face. It was so close he could smell the impact's burn. Screaming out, the raider turned and fled as a second shot shattered the glass door behind him. While Luc was scrambling towards the car, the owner appeared in the empty alloy frame, lifting his weapon for a third time. Sabine leaned over the roof of the car, spreading her legs, aiming carefully, and let off a string of nine millimetre shells that peppered the hunter's body, his head jerking skywards, blood spouting over the surprised curl of his mouth and thick, black moustache.

Luc turned just in time to see his assailant slump sideways against the door. Checking his stuffed pockets, he got up off his knees when he heard Sabine turn the ignition key. The engine rasped drily. Windows opened overlooking the scene. People began to gather. Some men picked up tools and charged. The car choked once more before it started, the girl swerving the steering wheel to avoid the cordon of vigilantes bearing down on them just as a wife's scream went up and the barking of a brown dog chased them out of town.

*

Costello was awakened at 6.55 when his SIS companion shook him by the shoulder. He came around in an instant, half out of bed, fingers instinctively clasping the pistol under his pillow. His dreams had been full of Sabine. He relaxed and grunted when he saw the face of the man standing above him. One glance at his wristwatch informed him it was time to push on.

They had been criss-crossing the countryside, avoiding wherever possible the *Mujahidin* troops, whose visibility seemed to increasing day by day. Costello's fear of cooperating with Fouvier's people was justified. Even the indignant and proud *Inspecteur* began talking openly about the scale of infiltration by the resistance inside his organisation.

'It gets worse and worse,' he would say privately. 'Every time there is an atrocity, a story about sex dens filled with white children, like the case at Cholet, the real French react.'

Costello nodded assent.

'Yes, the Cholet revelation is not helping us. There are similar situations in Marseilles but on a far larger scale. When such incidents break, there are bound to be questions asked about the benefits of sharing your country with such people.'

'I don't think "share" is the word many use now!' Fouvier whispered.

'I know, the scale of the forces landing in the south is overwhelming. They are also bringing heavy artillery.'

'President Belaire's last instruction was for all French military divisions to withdraw north of the Loire in an orderly fashion. The police are to hand over jurisdiction to the incoming forces.'

'Sounds like a calculated move.'

'I'm sure it is. A formal demarcation line like the one negotiated in Italy is a forgone conclusion.'

'And the population?'

'Safe passage north.'

'Any exceptions?'

'*Oui*. Children who are convertible to the faith!'

'Jesus!' Costello said.

'No. Allah!' Fouvier sighed.

*

The Citroen C5 VTR broke the far horizon just as the moon passed its feculent wind on the day, suffusing the leaves and branches of the surrounding chestnut trees with a ghostly life-force. Twenty kilometres further south, and the curve of the black metallic wing caught fire as dawn broke, sending a splash of blinding bright orange over the windscreen. Sabine felt the road pass smoothly under the vehicle's Michelin tread, rocking her gently back and forth. Luc met very little oncoming traffic, so he floored the accelerator and aimed straight for the onrushing sun.

Flies and moths splattered out in impact spots on the cold glass. Luc used the wipers to clear the windscreen as fresh morning air rolled in, hills and fields like a Van Gogh oil painting for kilometre after kilometre.

Once the sun had climbed above the windscreen, Luc pulled up to check the oil.

'I need to sleep,' he said rubbing his eyes.

They were on a vast plateau rutted with irrigation channels and covered by apple trees. The lines of the orchard's planting ran with the certainty of Roman cohorts to all compass points. While Luc lifted the hood, Sabine got out and leaned back against the car door, breathing in the fruity tang of the trees. Lighting up she bent down to apply mascara in the rear view, eyes squinting in wonderment at the sight over Luc's shoulder. A sandy brown wall dissected a vast orchard at right angles, forming a medieval compound. The grass moved in layers, brushing like an invisible comb through yellow hair, midges hovering in clouds of black muslin over drainage channels sunk in the earth.

Sabine's pupils shone wet like mischievous onyx. Without words, she took Luc's hand firmly in hers and they moved in tandem across the fields towards an archway in what Sabine began laughingly to call 'The Great Wall of China'. As they approached, they could see it was an old Catholic presbytery. The edifice had long since outlived its usefulness and been deserted by the monks. In the mildew of the masonry, wild spring flowers had started to bloom. They pushed on a chain gate and, after a persuasive creak and squeal, there was a grind of hinges and it gave way. Inside, they could see the secret sanctuary of a consecrated garden, once tended by diligent hoes, split in two by a stone path leading up to the chapel's ossified skeleton. Most of the roof had fallen in long ago and the buckling walls seemed to be held up by climbing ivy. The odour of silent decay was preserved there like a graveside vigil. Except for the chorus of small birds nesting in the nooks and crannies there was no life at all. When the intruders came closer, however, the swallows swooped down, filling the place with bird-call, trying to drive off the invaders.

Looking upwards they could make out the warped rafters that once formed the floor of the steeple attic. A green mossy bell still swung way up there beating tediously in communion with the wind. Slowly and steadily it tolled, marking time where time had lost its meaning. Circumnavigation of that petrifact of Christianity led to a section where a portion of sandstone had forward-rolled into rubble, covered by grime and millipedes. Together they scrambled through the hole into the inner sanctum. Inside a black rat suddenly broke cover and scurried before their faces. Sabine screamed when she saw its long tail and Luc seized a length of metal pipe and chased around after it for a while, beating at the ground in a vain attempt to silence the squeaking of sharp yellow teeth. In the end Luc fell to his knees, exhausted.

'Did you see that bastard go?' he stammered.

'Yes,' she said, 'I never saw anything move so fast in my life!'

Luc raised his head, watching the blue of her dress as Sabine picked her way through the maze of chafed slates and buckling columns around the altar.

'This must have been the pulpit,' she shouted pointing to a nest of ants hanging off a worm-eaten block of wood on the wall, 'and that's where ornaments like the cross and lectern were kept,' she pointed to what was now an empty belly of air.

The faint outline of the face of Christ on the one remaining piece of stained glass was covered by a layer of mould.

'Look,' she continued excitedly, 'you can still see the mosaic.'

Luc glanced in the direction of white doves and plum-faced cherubs lost in a sea of waving palm leaves.

'What's that he's sitting on? A camel?'

'An ass, you idiot! It's the Messiah entering Jerusalem.'

Luc sat on a pedestal, smoking marijuana. He spat out a lungful of green mucus that stung like battery acid as it seeped into a cut on his cupped palm.

'People used to seek sanctuary in places like this,' he joked.

Then, the thought of the car standing in open country bothered him. What if someone drove by and reported it? His mind was racing as he scrambled back through the wall and ran under the trees. Before he had covered half the distance, he fell to his knees. He got back to his feet, shaking his head, and walked slowly this time to where the car sat, exposed on the red dirt at the side of the road. In the distance a makeshift caravan of dispossessed French shuffled north, driven on by the bayonets of their conquerors, scavenging for food and scarce fuel.

He had already turned the key and circled the Citroen back across the fields, heading towards the presbytery, before his companion saw him coming through a breach in the stonework. Luc yanked the brake on the car just behind the wall, out of sight from the road. He went back into the secluded garden and lay down on an overgrown grave. Sabine came over and spooned herself around him and the two slept like a modern day Adam and Eve until the sun reached its zenith.

*

Said moved uneasily in his sleep. His wife, Rasheeda, tried to soothe him by stroking his sweaty back as she lay at his side in their bedroom. She knew about his nightmares: sometimes he confessed some of the images of the future haunting his subconscious.

In his fevered imagination, Ben Hassi often foresaw a time when inhuman behaviour had taken over, trees were cut down to feed the great fires of Nigerian parties, and cargo cult ceremonies on the Place Denfert-Rochereau. Weeds spread through streets and there were broken drains all over Place Charles de Gaulle. On the periphery of his vision he could sense the Sub-Saharan *vulgus* shimmying under the archways of derelict churches; Adva Cohen's people passed by in new cars on the way to beautiful and ancient synagogues; and Imams regaled their audiences in the plazas, lines and lines of kneeling worshippers trying to avoid the falling masonry from the Gallic skyline. Scattered here and there among the buildings were cellars where the infidels were held in the dark, brought out for Imam Taiyyab festivals, their bodies burning like roman candles in the town squares up and down the land. How long, he thought, before 'money-masters' like Cohen decided to use the multitudinous Nubian descendants to overthrow his new Egypt in Europe?

Sometimes Said thought that the prophet sent him such visions to test his resolve. It only made him more determined to enforce the new caliphate in the name of Allah and secure this land for his own offspring, rather than leave them languishing in the dust-bowl they had made of their own land.

*

Once again, they moved from safe house to safe house, edging ever southward towards the coast. The skeletal steel pylons carried overhead cables for kilometre upon kilometre across rolling, honey-coloured hills littered with Romanesque churches. As they walked gusts of wind sounded pennywhistle tunes on the bouncing wires, attracting birdsong. Luc and Sabine cut two lonely figures in the landscape, strolling hand in hand through the wheat-fields, talking about better times.

In a small village they came upon a war memorial surrounded by flowers. Sabine stood and read out the names etched around the stone figure of a soldier holding a Berthier above his head.

'That's a lot of men,' Luc said.

Sabine bowed her head, as Luc recited an excerpt from Pierre Drieu La Rochelle. 'Oh death, I do not forget you. Oh life truer than life. Oh unsayable thing that is beyond life and truer than life. Not beyond but within. It's the core of my being I want to attain.'

'Beautiful,' Sabine murmured.

'Yeah, and despised suicides like him led bayonet charges at Charleroi.

Feeling relatively isolated they lay low, paranoid about using any form of digital communication, aware that the telecom infrastructure was monitored by the intelligence services, microchips sparking into action the moment certain combinations of words were recorded. They had planned for this and maintained 'radio silence,' so to speak, conscious that they were among France's most wanted fugitives and that it was only the upheaval all around that allowed them the space and time to exploit government confusion.

*

Listening to the TV broadcasts and reading between the lines of newspaper reports gave them an insight into the unfolding of events:

> Versailles. A sympathiser had been narrowly prevented from firing on the Presidential car.

Brive. Mass protests at a sporting event leads to the seizure of the city council.

St-Omer. English Sceadugenga units are reportedly fighting alongside local resisters in the Bas de Normandie.

Vitrolles. A tenth teenage girl goes missing in the space of a week.

Troyes. Town Hall meetings are halted on the grounds they are not sufficiently focussed on Community cohesion.

Rotterdam. First public hanging of the new Millennium.

Paris. Government declares open borders policy a resounding success.

Chaumont. Young family burnt to death in South African style attack on isolated farmhouse.

Bruges. Bank robbery attributed to political rather than criminal gang

Tours. Inter-communal violence flares at religious site.

Loches. The whole catalogue of Nouvelle Droite books are pulped by order of the legislature.

Various. Trials of undesirable elements become too numerous to mention.

*

They took up residence in a musty, wooden garret in the fortified hilltop town of Belves. Every morning Sabine threw open the windows on a fine view over terraced gardens to the Nauze valley and felt almost compelled to scream with frustration.

Luc settled much quicker than Sabine into the rural rhythm and soon they had established a routine befitting a newly married couple, much to the amusement of their inquisitive neighbours, who smiled indulgently and imagined that the young wife was just broody for children.

One day there was a knock on the door and Sabine looked out from an upstairs window.

'It's Uncle Franck!' she called down to Luc who threw the bolt and opened up the house to his friend.

'Come in,' he said, 'It's really good to see you.'

They joined Sabine who had clattered down the stairs to meet them, Armalite in hand, congregating in the small back courtyard. Bodine noticed the waft of rotting vegetables coming from the dustbin as he squeezed Sabine's forearm.

'Looks like you are a regular young couple now,' he laughed, 'Any plans for kids?'

'The cover works a little too well. The old lady next door brings me organic potions to boost my fertility!'

Bodine's eyes twinkled sympathetically.

They threaded their way down the narrow garden path at the back of the house. An overgrown stone wall was covered in brown briar to their left, the backs of tall narrow houses rose all around them. The sun was hardly visible. Bodine thrust his hands into his jacket pockets trying to take it all in with one gulp of air.

'We need to make plans,' he eventually said as they sat around a small pond, sharing cigarettes.

Luc nodded. Bodine winked at the girl reassuringly. Sabine trailed her fingers in the water. Slowly small gold fish floated up, opening their mouths.

'They are pretty,' Bodine said.

'They are hungry,' Luc replied.

'I always feed them about this time,' Sabine said, wistfully. 'Now tell me what I want to hear.' *La Pétroleuse* blew blue breath with anticipation.

'Well, the command want you to stay underground,' Bodine started.

'But we discussed this when we were in Orléans. You said a few months to rebuild and we would become operational again.'

'I know, but there has been a change of plan.'

'Not from my point of view—our point of view, I mean!'

'Look this is bigger than a personal vendetta!'

'Is that what you think this is?'

'You are a symbol now. Our people venerate you like a modern-day Saint!'

'That's why I need to keep active!'

'*Non!*'

Sabine stopped short, stubbing her butt. 'Why?'

'Because your myth is a weapon in itself. We cannot afford to let you be captured or killed. If people think you are always out there they will have hope and that is what the resistance needs more than anything right now: hope.'

'So what are you advocating?' Luc said.

'We want to get you to Spain.'

'Spain?'

'We have friends around Bilbao willing to take you in.'

'You've already talked to them?'

'We are running a joint offensive with the Heol Telwen and they have very good links in the Basque territories.'

Sabine sat back and lit up another cigarette.

'How do we get there?' she asked. 'The country is crawling with informers and patrols.'

'We already have a car for you and a chain of supporters who can feed, clothe, and supply all your petrol.'

'Weapons?'

'Naturally!'

*

Said and Rasheeda waited like the excited grandparents they were for their son Najih and his wife Fatima's plane to land at the newly renamed Al-Yasa airport. Over two hundred flight arrivals and departures every day guaranteed the upper and middle class families from places like Amman, Muscat, and Khartoum did not have to rub shoulders with those from Benin, Angola, Chad, Djibouti, Gambia, Niger, and Senegal that came in via other forms of public transport. It was the largest mass exodus of all time and it was straining the country's humanitarian organisations to breaking point. Soup kitchens were organised for the starving, clothes collection centres for the semi-naked, and pre-ordered citizenship papers for the professional classes, all of whom came with their families and dependents in wave upon wave of multifarious colours, laughing and happy to have reached the chosen land of social security benefits, water, electricity, gas central heating, and pale and freckled boys and girls.

When Najih and Fatima emerged through customs, fast-tracked and unsearched because of their father's status, Said ran to embrace his grandchildren. He lifted Sahar and Waqas, thin brown limbs dangling in the air, kissing them passionately.

'Welcome to your new home!' he said, lovingly.

*

The police vans from out of Montelimar, supported by motorised columns in Nyons, set up a headquarters in a small village square. From the communications van, Fouvier issued instructions to his men to radiate outwards over a one-hundred kilometre area, rousing people from their beds and initiating beatings where they felt it may yield information.

One group came across a farmer's cottage in Privas. Gaston Cote stood defiantly in his doorway, pointedly refusing to cooperate with the detectives on his threshold.

'*J'ai vu rien, tu comprends*' he repeated, for twenty minutes or so. Snarling dogs circling the policemen's legs.

'Listen Gaston' the commander said, 'Do you want us to turn you over to the Berbers? You know they would love to get hold of Madame Cote,' he emphasised, pointing to the slim blonde thirty-year hold hovering in her chemise in the glow of their torch lights.

'You would do that?'

'We may have no choice. The barbouzers are in charge now; they have the whip hand.'

'But you are French?'

'So are they! Have you seen their passports?'

'Phew!' Gaston shook his head, 'This world is being turned upside down!'

The troopers forced their way past Gaston, taking him by the arms and pushed his wife to the ground, inserting a gun in her vagina.

'Check everything,' went the order, 'We have information this man is part of the trip-wire system back to *La Pétroleuse*.' Then, turning his attention to the restrained Gaston, the commander stated again, 'Now, have you thought of anything you wish to tell me?'

Le Sud

On the move again, they followed the migrating birds to the sea. The C5 was crossing salty flatlands, a terrain ribbed by sandy dunes. Distant river tributaries unwound like metallic cassette tape in the mist. Luc stopped the car on a levee and, taking off their shoes, they walked barefoot in the sand, splashing each other and scavenging amongst the spider-green thread of weed and popping air-pods, skipping flat stones out to a small harbour. For a while they shouted against the shoreline breeze and listened as their voices rebounded off craggy cliff walls.

When the wind turned chill at twilight, they made a fire and huddled together using the car as a windbreak. Luc checked his pockets. He had some money, but she was cleaned out. All the stores were closed so they could get nothing to eat. Their stomachs rumbled all night until they woke with splitting headaches, desperate for coffee and croissants.

Twenty minutes further along the coast road, they stopped at a shack and got some hot, black instant and a couple of chocolate bars. Driving on, they came across some beach houses, marching along the cliff tops like giant lobsters heading for spawning grounds.

As they came up close they could see the huts were closed for the season, empty windows staring back at them invitingly. Each chalet stood on wooden poles with a raised platform. The door to number five hung loose on its hinges and Luc used his shoulder to gain access. Crossing the threshold like newlyweds, they hit the light switch on a hallway and stepped onto creaking floorboards. A generator cranked into action. The rooms were dry and large. Off the hallway, to the right, were the bathroom, toilet and kitchen. To the left was a further bedroom, its large windows looking out to sea.

For the next four days Luc and Sabine did not leave the beach hut other than for a foray into town where they stole sufficient provisions to hold out for a week. They ate pasta and eggs around a farm table, smoked, and pondered the future. They slept in a big bed, with a fresh mattress and clean linen, taken from a huge pine wardrobe in the spare bedroom. At night, his fingers would slide inside the folds of her vagina, her eyes enlarging with the sensation, until they were almost fit to burst with orgasm. Afterwards, they would drop naked from the balcony, swimming out to sea, pointy chins breaking the water's surface under the moonlight.

Luc had hung around outside the kitchens of all the restaurants and hotels, and had eventually got himself a temporary bar job at La Plaza. The money was cash in hand and no questions asked, which suited them perfectly. He found that any spare food left lying around the kitchens was fair game and the

larder in the beach house was soon stacked with
poultry, claret, and yogurt. Sabine spent most of her
day reading some old leather-bound editions of
Barres and René de Chateaubriand's *Memoires
d'outre-tombe* that Arnaud Bellew had sent to her.

She recalled through rose tinted spectacles warm
September evenings spent out in the fields, her
arms and legs as brown as baked wholemeal bread.
She had played tag between the trees, Papa walking
Maria into the bushes and the Bertrand sisters milk-
ing cows in the yard. She could remember riding old
Pierre the donkey in the garden, his wide warm
flanks between her thin thighs as they plodded
along, watching the rabbits running over the
undulating hillsides. Her ears were full of the sound
of rushing streams and the laughter of boys, trousers rolled up to their knees, tickling trout from the
water. Mamma would buy them for a few Euro and
fry them in a big iron pan. She could almost smell it
still, her nose filling with the aroma of roasting al-
monds, herbs, and oils.

There was a true sense of nature's grand scheme
back then. Sentiments she later came across in the
pages of Péguy's *Notre jeunesse*. Her mother, her
father, all together drinking chocolate from big
white breakfast cups before she dressed for school.
She found herself drawn back to a passage in *Scenes
et doctrines*—'Human reason is linked together in
such a way that we all pass again in the steps of our
predecessors . . . We are the continuity of our parents. This is anatomically true. They think and they
speak in us. The entire series of descendants only
makes one and the same being.'

'That is why I am fighting,' she thought, 'for a future for our children!'

One afternoon, she had picked up a stick and
beaten a trail through the undergrowth at the back

of the hut. The boundary fence was a wire mesh, hung over wooden stakes. Luc had hidden the C5 under the overhang of some trees. Cars would occasionally pass by to the east of the property, but no one seemed to notice them. Perhaps the locals thought they had rented the place. She had only ever seen one man watching from across the fields. He was walking his dogs and collecting driftwood for the fire. It seemed they had achieved virtual anonymity, rent-free.

*

Said Ben Hassi appears on the steps of the Elysées Palace to confirm that the next round of Presidential elections will only apply to Departments north of the Loire

State laws now make it mandatory for women to wear the *hijab* in all areas with a majority Muslim population

Tax incentives encouraging non-Muslims to enter into arranged marriages with new male arrivals coming into the country are endorsed by the Counsel General.

*

Luc would come home late, jacket tossed over his shoulder, telling boring stories about work. Serving drinks at table Sabine would sit listening to him patiently as she cut slices of chicken and cheese.

'This is the best holiday I've ever had!' she was saying. Luc forked some ham stained with red vinegar into his mouth and lit a cigarette. Sabine got up from the table and closed the shutters on a rising westerly. Luc took a pack of cards out of his pocket.

'Game?'

'Sure!'

After two hours Luc threw his hand down on the table exhausted.

'You always win,' he complained.

'Lucky at cards, unlucky in love!'

'Let's go for a walk . . .'

Outside, the moonlight was just sufficient for them to make out the lizard eyes projecting out of rock pools. Clasping hands, they walked on into the night. A cruise ship, lit up like a Christmas tree, rocked to Latin rumbas in the bay. Sabine could see figures moving under a canopy of coloured bulbs.

'You know, when all this is over I'd like to take a job on one of those and just sail away.'

'Where to?'

'Argentina!'

'Why Argentina?'

'Because of Evita Perón.'

Disturbed by the blind fluttering of bats' wings, they returned to the hut in a playful mood. Fighting, they rolled onto the floor, arm in arm, and leg over leg like a giant knot of flesh. Open mouthed, they kissed, whispering to each other what they were going to do in bed before Luc threw her off, rising to make coffee. Sabine sat propped up in a wicker chair complaining that the seat made criss-cross patterns on her bare legs.

'You're always bitching,' he said. 'Drink this.'

In the early hours of the morning she got out of bed, drawn by something she could not explain—a sixth sense she had developed whilst they were on the run. The peninsula was often exposed to chill headwinds that drew mists in from the water. She picked up a smoke and flicking a Zippo lighter wandered past the table, collecting some binoculars as she stepped out onto the veranda. Leaning against the wooden rail she levelled her sights on the blurred division of sea and sky. At first, Sabine's eyes could see nothing, but then indistinct shapes began to emerge. Rafts and skiffs with single make-shift sails appeared on the water. She took the cold morning air deep into her lungs and after the tingle of the first breath she began to taste the stench of the Djebels sticking in the back of her throat.

*

The invaders came at Lembras in full force at dawn. The French watched them advancing behind a shower of shells. The Muslims were about two hundred metres from the outlying houses, tanks crashing through the fences and up the driveways towards the houses. Their troops were already fanning out to encircle the inhabitants. Costello had to twist and turn beneath a constant shower of incendiary devices and tracer fire. The Emir had set up his headquarters at Corbiac, a chateaux and vineyard that had been in the same family for nearly five hundred years. It stood overlooking the Grandval towards the river Dordogne. When he eventually consdescended to grant the British officer an audience, he met Costello's tired face with a contemptuous stare from an elegant armchair.

'Major Costello, by all the wealth Allah showers on his people, it is wonderful to see you!'

The Englishman nodded assent.

'Your men stopped me on the road to Bergerac.'

The Emir smiled. 'Yes I know!'

'But I am on government business. I have papers.' Costello offered them.

'I understand but you must realise circumstances change by the hour.'

The Briton tried to argue his case.

The Emir ignored him. 'Have you seen the curtains? Exquisite, are they not?'

'I'm sorry, Emir, but I really must insist . . .'

A lightning strike flashed across the domino face of the man on the leather throne.

'Insist? It is I who insists here!'

His legs swung over the side of the chair, dark fingers travelled thoughtfully over his moist lips.

'Sir, I am not questioning your authority.'

The Emir chuckled sarcastically and puffed out a thick cloud of cigar smoke.

'You are a *kuffar*!'

'I'm a representative of her Majesty's Government!'

His accuser smiled.

'Soon we will fly our flag over your Buckingham Palace.'

For the next two days he was questioned and intimidated by Bergerac's new Commissar, Jan Brossolette, a man rapidly gaining a reputation for diligent brutality. He was particularly concerned that his men did not kill their victims before they revealed the extent of their European networks. His Eurabic masters were trying to anticipate the capabilty in the Northern and Eastern European homelands of forces that might seek to oppose them. Brossolette and his type were mandated to replace people like Fouvier, who were considered 'old school.' Such mercenaries were motivated by cash and political advantage, vying for the attention of their new Berber overlords. Brossolette particularly enjoyed smashing kneecaps. He liked to hear the patella crack like a snail's shell. Then, he would look into his victim's wet eyes and take pleasure in the split bone shearing away. 'Talk,' he would say as he lifted the hammer once more. He was especially excited by the opportunity to capture *La Pétroleuse*. 'I will peel her skin,' he predicted. Once Costello was released, following a negotiated settlement involving an exchange of gold, the Englishman drove off through the retreating columns of white refugees. It reminded him of old sixties' and seventies' documentaries that showed footage of airports in Luanda and Lourenco Marques, where Europeans camped out in their hundredss, fleeing the bloodbaths that followed African independence. He was becoming increasingly concerned that it should be him that ended Sabine's life with a bullet. Anything to prevent her falling in to the hands of such people.

*

The bedroom door swung open filled by a large silhouette and two smaller snarling accomplices. Luc rolled over on his skinny shoulder and recognised the shapes of two fully grown bull mastiffs. A flashlight met his glare and the dog's claws scratched the bare boarding.

'Police patrol,' said the deeper shade of darkness behind the circle of light, 'Get your IDs ready.'

Luc reached under the covers and gripped Sabine's calf with a clammy hand. She came around slowly, still half stoned, to be confronted by drooling fangs. They lurched and almost snapped her face off. Her natural reaction was to scream and shrink back in abject fear. The beast, smelling its favourite human emotion strained at the leash, its dripping jowls cracking together only centimetres from her breasts. Sabine was driven back against the wall, dropping her bra, clinging to a blanket like a trapped matador. Luc noticed how the search beam lingered on her features, legs, and shoulders for a long time as he pulled on his Levis and T-shirt.

'Call those bastards off, for Christ's sake!' he screamed.

'Hurry up or I'll let them go,' came the reply.

Sabine had her knickers around her knees as she spoke.

'Look, we'll move on, we're just passing through . . .'

The hounds were rearing up on their hind legs. The policeman was struggling to contain them, their howling almost deafening.

'Caesar, Nero, easy boys!'

There was a moment's reprieve as the flashlight went *click* and died. Then, a second's pause and the main light went on.

'You know,' the officer began, much calmer now, watching the girl drop a shoulderless dress over her head, 'with a figure like that you could make a lot of money!'

'The oldest profession?' she smiled, reaching for a Marlboro from the bedside cabinet.

'Don't knock it. There are a lot of girls making good money around here off the foreigners.'

His eyes were greedily taking in the scene, not noticing Luc's hand lifting an Uzi from the tangle of bedsheets. Luc pulled the trigger, shredding both canine and pig flesh in a hail of rapid gunfire.

They scrambled down the hallway, bundling straight into the cop's partner, who had stepped forward after hearing the shooting. The officer got off a round at close quarters. Luc dropped to his knees clutching at a hole in his side. Before the policeman could finish the job, however, Sabine threw a knife, the blade slicing through his jugular and carotid. She walked slowly in the shadows of the corridor as her victim stood looking down at his stained flak jacket, drowning in his own blood. She then pulled the knife out and thrust it deep again, making sure he was dead.

Sabine turned, hauling Luc to his feet and they staggered forward, crimson beads trailing them across the boards. Outside, the police car radio was blaring out sports news. The engine was still running. Sabine ripped out the keys and threw them into the scrub. Jumping into the C5 they took off.

'Fuck, where do we go?' Luc said, between sharp, painful intakes of breath.

Sabine was loading a P90 submachine gun clamped tight between her thighs.

'We'll make a run for the border.'

*

Costello drew up at a small level crossing. Over the last hour he felt he had talked with every law enforcement department between Orange and Aix. Raised voices reported strong evidence that *La Pétroleuse* had been involved in a shoot out near Arles. Ahead, he could see two shafts of yellow light sparkle and glint off the iron rails. The night was dark and heavy. He had a gun on the passenger seat next to him. The sound of a thin metal bell ringing filled the evening air as the roar of piston wheels, chain-ganged down the track. He rubbed his cheek, as the train passed, privately congratulating himself that he had got this far without the interference of Europol militia or involving the mountebanks from the Maghreb in pursuit of his quarry. When the barrier began to lift and Costello slid into gear, eyeing his weapon, the car rolled forward into Provence.

*

A Tiger Attack helicopter soared overhead, its downdraft ripping loose the contents of rubbish bins by the road. Sabine listened as a second came in low over the flatlands from the east. In the command chopper John Costello followed the nod of the pilot's visor, recognising the car below as the signal that had seconds before appeared on the computer screen. Sabine D'Orlac was now a bleeping red dot at the centre of the black plasma. He looked down from the cabin and saw the speeding vehicle navigating the landscape below, tyres squealing. Then the Tiger banked abruptly, pulling around to the west as the car disappeared into an underpass through the mountains.

They circled overhead, waiting for their prey to reappear. As she emerged at the other end, Sabine pushed even harder on the accelerator. She wove wildly around the commuter traffic, a hubcap coming off, trying to shake off the predators moving through the tops of the trees. Perspiring and pale, Luc's face leaned against her shoulder, his eyes closed, his breathing laboured. Sabine had hastily treated his wounds, but the gauze was sopping and needed changing. As they sped along the highway Sabine leaned forward, attention fixed on the tarpaulins coming off the trucks swaying either side of them. She looked down the road ahead and saw a third Fennec Euro-copter rushing fast towards them. Sabine swerved violently to the right, grating along the barrier until she took out a whole panel in a spray of sparks and metal shards, crossing into the oncoming lane. She shrugged Luc off and began firing out of the sun roof, the C5 convulsing as she snaked between the roadside hoardings. She heard the swarm overhead closing in on them, buzzing like a hive of hornets. A drum roll of 30mm automatic fire from a Nexter cannon played across the

Citroën's bonnet and a spume of black oil spattered the windscreen. She tried the wipers but they spread greasy rainbows across the cracked glass. Nearly blind, she jammed on the brakes, searing the rubber, screeching to a halt only metres from an oncoming truck that jack-knifed over, tarpaulins fluttering upwards, like a great green sail that wrapped itself over the front of one of the choppers, causing it to bank sideways right into the path of another, in a cataclysmic impact.

*

Slowly, the fat black fly on the windshield came into focus. She could not unfasten her seatbelt, so she cut the strap with a knife and got out of the car to reconnoitre. The truck had pitched headlong into a ditch, its driver's head hanging loosely where it had snapped, dead eyes like poached eggs. Sabine saw the outline of a helicopter frame burning among the collapsing gantries of a water tower.

She stepped further from the car, a trapped animal in a dry landscape. Holding tight to the bruise under her left armpit she ran towards the second burning wreck. Steam and smoke was billowing from the cabin, bodies like dolls lolled in their buckled flight straps, trails of burning fuel creating rivulets of brown diaorrhea down the hillside.

Luc had come around and was following Sabine on stilted legs. The helicopters' wrecked fuselage had strewn technical entrails for over a kilometre. Despite his pain, Luc could just make out ahead her determined stride and her firm grip on the M1 carbine into which she had thrust a fresh clip of thirty millimetre shells.

The second copter was burning briskly. Pieces of cloth lifting in the heat, rising over the blackening bodies. When the fuel tank exploded on the Fennec AS550 spiked to the tower behind her, a curling red ball rolled along the phone lines bringing down the old wooden poles like matchsticks and streams of smoke poured forth around them. Luc ran towards the road as the remaining helicopter roared across the crash site, its rotors churning up a whirlpool of dry pine needles and plastic shopping bags. He shouted for Sabine, who was squatting in the shade of an upturned crate, ready to shoot. With a smile she duly obliged, sending up a *rata-tat-tat* of intermittent fire while Luc climbed into the cabin of the second chopper and prised a FAMAS G-2 assault rifle out of a dead man's grip.

*

The hot sunlight cast an oppressive weight across the scene. From the car radio they could make out Serge Gainsbourg singing *Je t'aime . . . moi non plus*. Luc threw Sabine a fractured smile; it reflected hers.

'They'll be back in a few minutes with more men,' he said, then jabbing through a hole in the C5's windscreen with his cigarette. 'There!' he shouted, 'Make for there!'

She twisted her wrist to start the ignition, span the wheel to get the car back onto the road, making for the cover of a block of half-constructed apartments standing in a field about two kilometres away.

They hurriedly emptied out the boot, running back and forth, transferring armfuls of contraband munitions, a Heckler and Koch 33, a Danish Madsen, an Armalite M16, and a scratch handled Ingram with an elongated silencer.

Meanwhile, Costello was still in the helicopter, hovering nearby, calling Fouvier for reinforcements.

Sabine swung Luc back towards cover and pulled a leather flying jacket over her shoulders. At the top of the stairs they ran into a labyrinth of dark corridors. Luc steadied himself on a wooden rail as the helicopter appeared over the thin line of pine trees marking the complex's southern perimeter. He stared up at the young woman rushing ahead in the maze, firing out at the daylight every time she came to an empty window. He thought they were like rats in a trap.

As they entered the top apartment, Luc almost lost consciousness. He staggered, semi-delirious, shoulder hitting the wall, eyes a murky blur. He watched the young woman's curves on the grey plaster ceiling as she moved about the rooms, placing ordinance in strategic positions.

As she leaned against the concrete parapet, gun barrel tracing the flight of the helicopter sweeping in low over them, Sabine felt Luc's hands grip her bra strap. She turned to find his rigid face right next to hers, the corner of his mouth trickling blood and his sunken eyes clouding as the death mist slowly descended. A car moved along the perimeter. She let off a few shots, taking out the windscreen and forcing the vehicle off the road into a small copse. Lieutenant Bruyere and some of his men returned fire, bullets chipping at the stonework around their quarry. Sabine laughed, disengaging herself from Luc. She eased the pin on a hand grenade and forced it into his trembling hands. She pressed his thumb down on the detonating cap.

'Keep that pressure there,' she instructed, 'do you understand?'

He nodded before staggering back through the apartment, sliding down the wall adjacent to the entrance.

'We've got no water?' he said after a long silence.

'Non,' she confirmed.

Her eyes were looking out at the iron ring encircling them as the first flicker of twilight settled on the near-arid landscape. Appeals from Inspector Fouvier for them to surrender were met with Sabine's 'Go fuck yourself!'

*

Sabine stood on guard, staying away from the windows in case they had snipers armed with infra-red. She remained motionless, back against the wall, scanning the room for a long time as Luc drifted in and out of consciousness, freezing at the slightest sound. She was trying not to breathe and was straining to hear what was going on in the building. Sure enough, they were already inside. She could hear chunks of brick crunch underfoot as Sebastian Bruyere rode point, making his way up the stone staircase, closely followed by a squad of men in full body armour. Moving quickly, she passed Luc, - warning him with a gentle kick.

'You've got to focus!' she said, and gestured for him to prime his device.

She then made it silently to the landing on her stomach. The oncoming footsteps had reached the last stairwell directly below her and Bruyere had placed his boot on the final flight.

Six more steps, she thought, and they will be here. Her heart almost stopped. She did not want to fire and reveal her position, so she unsheathed a knife, clutching it in both hands, and rose to her full height as the lieutenant came into view around the corner, signalling with his fingers for his men to come up. She rushed forward quickly, driving the blade down hard between his helmet and breast pad. Falling backwards, his gun ripping off a whole magazine in the deafening darkness, he skittled the others in the corridor. Bodies bounced down the echoing stonework. Taking advantage of the situation, Sabine fired from the top of the landing and was able to kill two more with the Heckler and Koch.

The stairwell was now deserted, but men had scaled the walls and were clambering in through the windows to the room behind her. She could not hide anymore. She ran forward, firing from the hip, shadowy figures dropping all about her. Entering the room she bent down low, like she had been taught, and circled like a wolf, snapping at its own tail, letting out a hail-storm of lead, taking out the troopers who had fanned out into recesses. When she ran out of ammo, she looked over to Luc, who was crouching in the corner. Their eyes met in knowing recognition across the room and he lifted his finger on the pin. There was a flash and an explosion that sent dust everywhere.

When she came around, Sabine stared incredulously at the spots of blood splashed on her bare legs and cotton dress. She stepped over a melange of severed limbs and steaming intestines, her foot slipping on a pancreas that had come out of the side of a torn torso, gliding across the floor in a mix of mucus and excrement. She could not hear anything. Both ear drums had been blown. Falling on her knees she vomited, then wiped away the snot from her nose, still reaching out for the Ingram with the full curling clip.

She was ready for them as they came through the breach in the wall, firing wildly, bullets ricocheting everywhere. The first two went down before they could even focus on her slim figure. Red beams tracking up the walls as black rubber boots bounced off the floor. The third got off a sweeping burst of nine millimetre shells which sawed Sabine's abdomen in half, throwing her back against the wall, finger still on the trigger and still firing. There was a snap as her spinal column gave. A bolus of thick green phlegm dribbled over her jaw and with dilated doll-like eyes Sabine slid down, jetting wide arcs of arterial blood to the floor.

*

Later, as John Costello waited to erase the evidence of the fire-fight, he saw a helicopter rising into the sky, a black helmeted pilot with a top-owl weapon sight at the controls, before it shrank away into the distance. Within a half hour, Fouvier's small procession of cars pulled off after collecting their trophy photographs and the terrorists' DNA. Costello watched them go with no particular regret. When they had finally disappeared over the rise, he turned to face the corpses of Sabine D'Orlac and Luc Dubois forming a small tableau of crucified martyrs on the veranda. He lit up a cigarette, let out a smoky sigh, and leaning back against the balustrade, he recalled the first time he had met the infamous *Petroleuse*, one night in Paris. A sea breeze caught his hair, brown wisps fluttering. The cicadas were the only soundtrack to his private vigil in the sunset.

Epilogue

The moonlit water lapped gently against the sides of fibreglass boats. Just ahead, beyond the foaming breakwater, the commandos, wearing their tricolor shoulder flashes, could make out the round topped silhouettes of sand dunes running away through the sea mist.

Dawn approached as the flotilla drifted a few hundred metres off the coast of Normandy. Night vision binoculars straining, waiting for the pinprick of infrared to signal it was safe for landfall. When it came, three quick blinks and a long flash, the boats' occupants checked their weaponry one final time, pulled their black balaclavas tight down over their determined pale faces, and waved encouragement before motoring into the shallows. Disembarking they slid their craft into camouflaged hiding places and zig-zagged up the beach to join their comrades sheltering in the shadows of the rocky overhang.

Franck Bodine welcomed them with undisguised joy. '*Pour terre et peuple.*'

'*Pour Luc et Sabine!*' came the reply.

They set out in single file across the pebbled clefts, dropping towards the bocage of fields beyond, disappearing into a landscape of yellow primroses and foxgloves towards Rouen, where the insurgents were regrouping against the occupation of their land.

FIN

ABOUT THE AUTHOR

Fenek Solère writes novels in the tradition of the New Right. In addition to *The Partisan*, he is the author of *Rising!* (2017), *Kraal* (2019), and *Resistance* (2021). He has published articles at *Counter-Currents*, *Defend Europa*, *New European Conservative*, *European Civil War* and *Patriotic Alternative*.

Lightning Source UK Ltd.
Milton Keynes UK
UKHW010813310322
400890UK00002B/245